RETISHELLA AND PIRATE COOL

To Matthew

Linda Bond

Linda Bond

X

Chapter 1

Coolibar Barrett pulled his ragged black coat tighter around his bony body. At this moment he was too cold to feel like a menacing pirate. The November wind blew strong and chill on the rocky beach and it made him shiver and wish he was at home with his mum. His thoughts returned to his captain, Jellycoe Jack, and the very important mission he had commanded everyone to join.

"See this 'ere map me stinking shipmates?" Jack had sneered, flapping a scrap of yellow paper at the crew assembled on the deck of the Mardy Meg in the clear frost of dawn.

"This map has passed through the hands of several dead pirates before it got to me." He traced a line across his throat as he spoke, and the pirates in the crowd winced at the thought. He lowered his voice and continued, "It tells me that if we can find a green shiny rock shaped like a pyramid, the 'normous treasure of Obscurity Island will be ours." He waited for a reaction from his crew but they just

3

stared in silence until he finished. "Don't you see, you brainless baggages? We'll all be treeemendously rich, yes treeemendously rich!" He turned and cuffed the ears of the pirates nearest to him, who ducked, despite trembling with the cold. They were not impressed. They had heard this promise many times before.

"Now set to you tiny turtlebrains and find me that rock or ye'll all be swabbing the deck with your tongues!"

Coolibar was puzzled. "Please Captain Sir, what is a pyramid?" The other pirates had turned to go and search but stopped in their tracks when they heard Coolibar speak. Jellycoe Jack did not like questions, even sensible ones.

"You mangy maggot!" He lashed out with the leather whip he always kept in his belt. The pirates leant back out of the way and no one was hurt. Jellycoe Jack continued, speaking to all the pirates, but looking directly at Coolibar.

"Think to make an idiot out of Captain Jellycoe Jack do you? Of course you know what a pyramid is, everyone knows." He cast a suspicious eye over the other pirates.

"Which one of you flaky fish-faces doesn't know what a pyramid is?"

The other pirates muttered among themselves.

"Ha ha!" sneered Garston Bones the quartermaster. "The lad doesn't know what a pyramid is!" The crew nervously joined in with Garston Bones' scornful laughter.

Coolibar was not so sure he believed any of them, not even Jellycoe Jack. As they all slunk off to at least pretend they were trying to find a green shiny rock in the shape of a pyramid, Garston Bones caught hold of Coolibar's sleeve, and snarled in his ear.

"It doesn't matter if you know what a pyramid looks like or not, boy," his hot, sour breath condensed on Coolibar's hair and dripped down his neck. "What ever you find on this island is to be reported to me straight away. Understand?" he twisted Coolibar's arm until his shoulder blade cracked. Coolibar winced with pain and nodded. He knew it was folly to ever cross Garston Bones. That's why the crew's nickname for him was 'Ghastly'.

He thought back to the day two years ago when his bad luck began. In the seaside town where he lived it was quite common to see sailors of all ranks off duty and wandering around town looking for food, drink, somewhere to stay, or just plain seafarer's fun. Indeed his own father was a merchant seaman, although neither he nor his mother had seen him for ten years, and as he was a baby at the time his father disappeared, his memories of him were blurred and brief. His only image of his father came from a fading picture his mother kept in pride of place on the mantelpiece.

That fateful day had started well. His aunt and uncle were on holiday and decided to stop off and visit them as they passed by on their journey.

His mother was a slight, gentle and kind lady who loved singing. His earliest memories of her were of her thin, high voice warbling nursery rhymes and folk songs learned at her mother's knee. She was singing a ballad about a girl called Nancy as she polished and tidied before her visitors arrived.

He sniffed and wiped away a tear, remembering the smell of lavender polish and the brightness of the sunlight through the open sash window. His mother's voice echoed in his mind like someone talking in the next room.

"Coolibar my dear, get yourself down to Brag's and buy us one of those lovely jam and cream sponge cakes for your aunt and uncle's visit. And don't be too long about it, they'll be here soon."

He remembered taking the shiny coin his mother offered him and walking down the narrow alley to the baker's shop. But before he reached the end of the alley everything went black as a group of Jellycoe Jack's pirates stuffed him into a rough hessian sack. From the inside as he struggled he felt a sharp pain on the back of his head. Then nothing.

When he woke it was dark. After the stinging pain pounding round the back of his head, the first thing he noticed was the smell. It was vile. Like a pan of boiled cabbage mixed with stinking cheese and unwashed underwear. He wanted to be sick.

"It's OK, lad, it gets us all like that at first. You'll get used to it."

Coolibar squinted as his eyes became accustomed to the smoky light from a nearby oil lamp. The gentle words came from a tall, lanky man with a mouth full of huge teeth that sparkled with gold when he smiled.

"Where am I?" Coolibar asked weakly, trying once again not to retch.

"You're on the Mardy Meg. It's a pirate ship."

Coolibar tried to get up, but the throbbing in his head and the lurching of his stomach overpowered him and he slumped back down into the hammock.

"It's no good trying to get away," continued the kind pirate. "We're well out to sea now, heading for another wild goose chase after a rumour of treasure on an island somewhere in the middle of this here ocean."

He mopped Coolibar's head with a cloth and gave him some water to drink.

"Better?" he asked. Coolibar nodded his thanks.

"What's your name boy?"

"Coolibar Barrett" came the weak reply.

"Unusual name for a lad," the pirate smiled.

"Yes," Coolibar agreed. "It was my mother's idea. Before she married my father her surname was Coolihan, and my father's is Barrett. She just split them both in half and stuck two of the halves together to make my name. Coolibar. You get used to it after a while. What about you?"

"My name is Bartholomew Nelson," he explained grandly, "but everyone here calls me The Admiral a'cos of me surname, you know Nelson, Admiral Nelson," he chuckled to himself, enjoying the joke.

Coolibar nodded again, but understood very little.

That day was the start of his new life. A life of keeping your head down and trying to stay out of trouble. That usually meant keeping out of the way of Jellycoe Jack. Or even worse, making sure you didn't bump into Ghastly.

He rubbed the still-fading scars on the back of his legs as he remembered his first meeting with Jellycoe Jack and Ghastly, the day after waking up on board. The Admiral had taken him to dinner with the other pirates for the first time. Dinner that evening consisted, as always, of dry black bread and stew. The pirates had learnt to eat first, ask what was in the stew later. Looking down at the frothy brown liquid with fatty lumps floating on the top, Coolibar understood why.

When everyone had been served, Captain Jellycoe Jack appeared, to say grace and make sure everyone was enjoying their meal.

"Who have we here?" Jack demanded in a menacing tone.

"This be the lad we picked up at the last port o' call captain," The Admiral explained.

"Has he a tongue in his head Master Nelson?" Jack sneered. "Boy, what is your name?" he poked Coolibar in the ribs with a bony finger.

"Please sir," Coolibar tried to keep his voice steady, but he was very afraid. "My name is Coolibar Barrett, sir."

"Crooli what?" Jellycoe Jack stammered.

"Coolibar sir, Coolibar."

"Well then Coolerburr. Whatever kind of stupid name is that?"

Coolibar looked down and studied his feet so the captain couldn't see that he had been hit by a bad case of nervous giggles, caused by seeing a grown up who couldn't pronounce his name, and the feeling of fear that prickled in his stomach as he realised he was standing before a fierce pirate captain, stuck out at sea miles from home. He didn't know why it made him laugh but it did. Not a normal, happy kind of laughter, but the kind that you do instead of crying.

The other pirates stopped their eating and talking and stared at Coolibar in shocked silence.

"Are you laughing at me you little louse?" Jellycoe Jack shouted in Coolibar's face, and Coolibar couldn't be sure if he was red through anger or embarrassment.

Coolibar shook his head, forcing his mouth to look serious. He didn't dare speak or he would have given the game away by sniggering.

"Well so long as you are one of my pirates, working for me, on my ship you shall be known as Cool. That's more of a pirate name than your fancy Coooolibilliation."

"Yes sir," Coolibar repeated but couldn't suppress a giggle.

"Mockery will not be tolerated on my ship!" Jack shouted so loud that Coolibar was sure the whole ship fell silent, as everyone aboard feared for him and for themselves.

"Garston Bones you will take this gormless giggler out of here and give him ten lashes of your fiercest cat o' nine tails. That should cleanse him of his insolence and teach him a bit of respect."

"My pleasure Captain," Ghastly sneered. "I'll enjoy the exercise."

Ghastly made sure that the beating put Coolibar into sick bay for a week.

From that day on everyone called him Cool. He got used to it after a while.

The crew spent most of their time following Jellycoe Jack's orders in the hope of finding something worthwhile somewhere in the endless expanse of blue sea. In the many months since Cool joined the Mardy Meg there had been countless rumours of treasure buried on islands in every ocean in the world. So far none of the rumours proved true and life on the Mardy Meg continued in the same hard and cruel routine. His only real friend on board was The Admiral, who helped him keep out of trouble and warned him when Ghastly or Jellycoe Jack was on the warpath.

In the evenings, after their disgusting dinners Cool and The Admiral would find a quiet spot on the ship and The Admiral would play him music on his English Concertina. For Cool it was a little ray of sunshine in the bleakness of life on the Mardy Meg.

One evening as they were settling down for a bit of relaxing music after a particularly greasy and sicky-smelling stew, Cool looked over to The Admiral, who was playing and looking at a piece of paper with printed dots in a strange pattern.

"What are you looking at?" asked Cool.

"Music, it's music written down," The Admiral answered.

"But you haven't used music written down before, you normally just remember the tunes you have heard," continued Cool.

"Yes," replied The Admiral. "I have been collecting tunes in my head for as long as I can remember. Collected them from far and wide, wherever I finds people playing music I tries to keep it alive in my memory and on my concertina."

"So what's different this time?"

"This piece of music the captain found among a bunch of letters and maps on the last ship we defeated. He didn't know what it was, but I recognised it."

"How is it that you can read music?" asked Cool.

"My father gave me this concertina on my tenth birthday," said The Admiral with a faraway look in his eye. "He was a great musician, could play the violin just as good as those lah-di-dah orchestra players. He could read music and he taught me. He used to say music is very powerful. It can make a man laugh one minute, and cry the next."

"Play it for me," said Cool, smoothing out the piece of paper and laying it in front of The Admiral. With a smile of pleasure he started to play.

"Do you know what it's called?" asked Cool when he had finished.

"No, the title is smudged and ripped."

"I think I recognise it," said Cool with a grin. "My mother used to sing a song with a tune like that. She called it 'Hearts of Oak' and said it was my father's favourite song."

"Do you know how it goes?" asked The Admiral, starting to play the tune again.

"No, but I remember the chorus," replied Cool, joining in:

"Hearts of Oak are our ships; Hearts of Oak are our men;

We always are ready; Steady boys, steady
14

We'll fight and we'll conquer again and again."

When The Admiral had finished playing they both fell to laughing and Cool let the soothing sound of a slow air followed by a rousing hornpipe wash over him, allowing him to escape the reality of life on the Mardy Meg, if only for a little while.

Chapter 2

As Cool wandered along the bay in the strengthening wind, the truth dawned on him and shrouded him with despair. He was marooned with the other pirates on the Mardy Meg. A prisoner of Jellycoe Jack and Ghastly Bones. He longed more than anything else to get away from the slavery of life on the Mardy Meg and return to being a normal boy again. He forced his wistful thoughts out of his wretched brain and thought of a plan. If there really was treasure on Obscurity Island and he found it, maybe he could talk the captain into sending him home. It was worth a try.

He looked out just beyond the bay where black storm clouds were brewing over white-crested waves. The Mardy Meg was dipping and rolling about on the swelling grey sea. He reminded himself of Jellycoe Jack's instruction "We meet back at this bay round midday, for we must drop anchor by night fall on the other side of the island."

Cool stamped his feet to try and keep warm. The wind was icy and howling. As he listened he realised it wasn't just the wind he could hear and he looked around the beach to find out where this strange mix of shrieking and singing was coming from.

On a seaweed-covered rock bathed by the incoming tide was a young girl, singing a strange screeching song and smoothing down her green hair with a shiny comb. Her glistening tail sparkled the colour of emeralds and sapphires. Cool stood and gasped, suddenly aware that he was looking at a real, live mermaid.

He couldn't stop staring, as if he was under some kind of spell. He noticed that each time the mermaid squealed louder the wind blew stronger and each time she squawked softer storm clouds scuttled across the sky.

Cool shook himself out of his trance, and as he forced his legs to move he tripped on a stone. The mermaid turned and glared at him with eyes the same colour as the stormy grey sea, and then she slipped off the shiny rock into the water.

At first Cool thought he must have dreamt it, he wondered if it was a trick of the light. But something glittery twinkled at him from the rock the mermaid had been sitting on. Cool paddled over in the foamy tide to take a closer look.

On the rock was a small rectangle of gold with long points like teeth running along one edge.

Cool gingerly reached out a hand to lift it off the green seaweed and held it up to the light.

"It looks like a comb; it must be the mermaid's comb." He turned it over in his hand, astonished by the delicate workmanship.

The comb was marked with strange squiggles like a kind of writing. Cool had been taught to read, but could not understand the squiggles on the comb. It was decorated with tiny sparkly shells that changed colour as you twisted it about in the light. A sound from behind him made him quickly hide it in his pocket.

"Hoy there Cool", it was Jellycoe Jack and the rest of the pirates. "Found anything today beetle-brain?"

"Wh-wh-what do you mean?" stammered Cool.

18

"Shiny green rock, boy, tha-ats what I mean" he answered, cuffing Cool round the head.

"Oh, oh, n-n-no," answered Cool, ducking.

"I've searched the whole of this bay," he added. "No shiny green rocks, only grey and brown ones."

The other pirates all agreed.

"Dozy dogbreaths!" cursed Jellycoe Jack. "That'll be half rations for you all tonight, and count yourselves lucky to get anything at all." The pirates didn't know whether to laugh or cry. Half rations of stew was a godsend, but a slice of stale bread and a rind of mouldy cheese weren't going to fill anyone's stomach.

"Get aboard the ship smartish, chicken-chested chumps!" Jellycoe Jack demanded. He looked up at the sky and sniffed the salty air. "We must set sail soon," he continued, "bee-cause what you mound of mushy mushrooms can't see is that we needs to get to Shelter Bay on the other side of this island where we can find better protection from the coming storm."

Back on board the Mardy Meg, Cool lay in his hammock waiting to be called to duty with the other pirates already battling with strong winds and choppy waves in an effort to leave this exposed coast find safe anchorage in Shelter Bay. He nervously put his hand in his pocket. The comb was still there. As he touched it he heard the wind screech even louder than before. He quickly took his hand out of his pocket and lay for quite a while wondering about the mermaid and the comb until he fell asleep, the ship rocking and rolling in the angry sea.

Chapter 3

Retishella mermaid was in a terrible panic. She was in dreadful trouble and didn't know who to turn to. She trawled through her memory of the day's events to see if she could remember how she had ended up in such a mess. Maybe then she would be able to change things.

She thought back to this morning, when she visited the storm-making rock, sitting on a cushion of green seaweed on a ledge in the side of the great rock, her tail dipping into the incoming tide.

She had come to wish her father a happy birthday in the traditional way, by sitting on the storm-making rock and singing a song for him. His favourite was the grey boomer song, and as she sang she marvelled at the speed with which she could move the grey globs of cloud around the sky.

"He'll love this one" she remarked proudly.

A sound like a pebble being kicked across the beach behind her made her turn around and take a deep breath of surprise.

Staring back at her was a skinny landish boy in a blue coat and trousers. He looked about her age but she sensed a great sadness surrounding him like a fog. He started walking backwards, legs slipping and stumbling on the damp pebbles, still staring at her open-mouthed.

"No, wait," she said and started singing the dream song. She had always been told that where there were landish people there was always danger for merfolk and she knew she had to get away.

Sooner than she expected, his bright blue eyes turned dreamy and she slipped into the foamy tide, and swam back out to sea giggling to herself.

"Landish people are so easy to fool," she thought proudly. "Strange though," she continued, "I had always been told landish people were ugly. He had the most beautiful blue eyes, although his muddy brown hair was disgusting."

She took a look at her own hair and was embarrassed to see flecks of pink, the colour of a mermaid blushing. She reached for her comb to smooth them out before anyone saw them.

But her comb was gone. For most mermaids this wouldn't have been a problem. For Retishella, her comb was more important than a way of keeping her hair tidy. She felt neither clever nor embarrassed now. Just scared.

"Oh great Spirit of the Sea," she begged under her breath, "Please don't let me lose my comb. It is my cordella."

Each merbaby chooses a cordella, a precious object that they must carry with them at all times. It is presented to them by the Spirit of the Sea in a most solemn ceremony that celebrates the time when they grow from merbaby to mermaid or merboy. It marks a merperson out as belonging to a certain village, clan and family, and gives them a place in the undersea world, a sense of history and identity. As they grow the power of the Spirit of the Sea inside it helps to develop their feelings and their ability to read the emotions of others.

Retishella's cordella was made of pure sea-gold from the deepest sea-gold mines. Her father had given her some trinkle shells, tiny sparkling spirals that change colour as the light catches them. He had ridden the fastest dolphins to reach the trinkle shell beds on the bottom of the Torzig Ocean, and to celebrate his pride at his little baby finally becoming a mermaid, her father had mounted the trinkle shells on her comb himself.

Without it Retishella knew she would be shunned. No other merperson would be allowed to talk to her, or even be seen with her. Not even her own parents. But more important than that, from the moment she was separated from her village, she would gradually lose the ability to change the colour of her hair and eyes and show others how she was feeling. Until she found it again she would not be a complete mermaid.

She slumped on the seabed and cried blue tears. She felt she had let the whole world down.

"Retishella, this won't do," she scolded herself. "You must search for it." She swam in a panic over to the storm-making rock, which by now was almost swamped by the tide, but her cordella and the landish boy were gone. She spent ages searching the rock, lifting the seaweed and feeling in all the nooks and crannies. Eventually she realised she would have to return home without it, dejected and fearful blue from head to tail.

"Retishella my maid," said her father laughing and enfolding her in a big hug. "Thanks for the grey boomer. It was a great birthday present." He noticed the mood his daughter was in and asked gently "Whatever is the matter maid? Are you sick or something?"

"Oh father what shall I do?" cried Retishella; "I've lost my cordella by the storm-making rock".

Her father's hair and eyes drained to grey then blue, as it slowly dawned on him that his daughter was in serious trouble. He knew that a mermaid must never be separated from her cordella.

Her father sat her on his knee and stroked her hair, which soothed her while she told him exactly what had happened. They returned to the storm-making rock and searched together but in the end had to report the missing cordella to Glorishell, the head of the village.

Later that day, as the clouds from the grey boomer covered the weak winter sun, the whole village returned to the storm-making rock, a throng of distressed blue hair and eyes at the last place Retishella remembered having her cordella, to perform the separating ceremony. Retishella was allowed to take nothing with her, no food or drink, not even her Dolphin King Stone. Everyone was feeling gloomy, but they had no choice. The Merlaws were very clear.

Glorishell read from a spiral of writing on an ancient rock. "Retishella, you have lost your cordella and are to be separated from this merclan until you find it again." The gathered people of the merclan sang together sorrowfully:

Go and swim the furthest oceans

Dive the deepest seas alone

Until you find your lost cordella

We will wait to welcome you home.

As a final parting gift, Mersia, the wise mermaid, touched the storm-making rock and hummed a dark tune. She stared at Retishella with a glassy trance in her eyes and spoke slowly and seriously.

"Your cordella is in a place near here, in the pocket of a landish boy on a ship made from trees and cloth. The landish people on this ship are also searching for something precious on the island by this storm-making rock. You must be quick Retishella; for once they find what they are looking for they will leave this place for ever." She reached out and handed Retishella a charmstone with a carving of the storm-making rock and some strange marks like writing. "When you find him" she explained, "tell him the information he is looking for is on this stone. You must then insist that he swap it for your cordella."

The villagers sang the separating song again and disappeared beneath the waves, leaving Retishella alone on the storm-making rock to sing a deep blue song and watch the beautiful blue colour of her hair slowly drain to a disgusting sludgy brown.

Chapter 4

The moaning wind and the lurching movement of the ship woke Cool up. He looked around at the other pirates wondering if they had noticed a change in the weather but they were all sleeping soundly on various makeshift beds and hammocks.

The wind sighed and to Cool it sounded like it was swirling on the deck of the Mardy Meg above his head. The teeth of the mermaid's comb were sticking into his leg through his trousers. He took it out of his pocket and turned it over in the dim light of the oil lamp. He thought it less shiny than before and the little shells looked duller. As he rubbed it against the leg of his trousers to try and polish it up a bit, he heard the wind whistle around the ship from bow to stern, a high, angry screeching like someone outside trying to get in. He stowed it away in his pocket quickly as he heard Ghastly climb down the rickety rope ladder into the hold where the pirates slept.

"What have you there my boy?" Ghastly reached out and grabbed Cool by the neck of his shirt, at the same time reaching into the boy's pocket to find the comb.

"Ow!" he exclaimed. "Whatever it is, it bit me!" He sucked a pinprick of blood from his finger and tightened his grip on Cool, making him gag.

"Take it out lad. Take it out and show me what it is."

Cool reached slowly into his pocket and pulled out the comb. As he did a low moaning wind seemed to seep in through all the nooks and crannies of the creaking ship. Cool thought he saw a glimmer of panic in Ghastly's eyes.

Ghastly snatched the comb from Cool's hand and studied it with a shudder. Cool sank back into his hammock as Ghastly's thick fingers released the grip on his neck. Some of the pirates close by began to stir from their sleep. Ghastly glanced furtively around the hold, and held the comb to his body, hiding it with his hands.

"Come with me boy," he demanded, pulling Cool roughly by the hand and back up the rope ladder.

On deck the wind was wheezing and insistent, puffing up the pirates' clothes, spitting salt water into their faces and tugging at their hats and hair.

"Where did you find this?" he demanded.

"Pardon, sir?" said Cool, finding it hard to hear anything in the screaming wind.

"Where did you…" Ghastly began, and then realising the stormy wind was snatching away his words and Cool couldn't hear him, he took hold of the boy's collar and frog-marched him into his quarters on deck.

Through the four portholes that punctuated the walls in Ghastly's spacious living quarters Cool could see the angry rhythmic rolling of the waves, white horses topping each rising crest. He realised they hadn't moved from the bay they were exploring earlier, they hadn't made it to Shelter Bay.

Ghastly pulled him around to look him square in the face.

"So, boy, tell me where you found this thing," he leant close to Cool and shoved the comb before his eyes.

"I found it on the beach," answered Cool, "This morning out in the bay by the seaweed-covered rock."

"You were told to report anything you found on that beach to me! Who do you think you are to defy an order from Garston Bones?" Ghastly lifted a hand to cuff Cool around the head. But he once again scratched his hand on the comb.

"Stupid thing!" he roared. He put his oily head next to Cool's and lowered his voice to a terrifying growl. "Well Cool, was there more treasure like this on the beach? Tell me boy, tell me at once!"

"No, I didn't see any more, only this comb," stammered Cool, wondering what Ghastly was up to. "I mean, there was nothing like a treasure chest, or anything, that's all."

"I hope you wouldn't lie to me boy," he threatened, "Or things will be very bad for you."

There was a roar of wind outside the ship and it lurched suddenly, sending them both stumbling across the cabin. Ghastly pricked himself with the comb once more. He tucked it away in his jacket pocket.

"Did anyone else see you pick up this comb?" Ghastly demanded.

"No," replied Cool truthfully, "I was the only person there."

"Good," Ghastly started to back away from Cool. "Keep it that way, or it'll be worse for you."

"Yes sir, I understand sir," replied Cool.

Ghastly lifted a hand to slap the boy, but instead he jumped in surprise and yelped with pain.

"There's something strange going on here," he snarled. "I don't know what it is, but I'm going to make sure you are just where I can find you until it is sorted out."

As he spoke, he picked up a piece of rope that he kept neatly coiled in the corner of his quarters 'just in case'. He used it to tie Cool to his big four poster bed.

"Don't try and move from here my lad," he threatened, "Or you will regret it like you have regretted nothing before in your life."

He turned to leave and Cool curled himself up on the floor of the cabin as much as the ropes would allow, feeling frightened and miserable.

He lay there for some time, listening to the wind becoming wilder and louder. He felt the movement of the Mardy Meg, at first just a rhythmic rocking that became more and more violent like a rollercoaster ride, until the ship seemed to be tossed and turned all ways, out of control and terrifying.

Above his head he heard the sounds of pirates jumping into action. He imagined them fastening the sails and tying down anything that could get swept overboard in the fierce storm.

Cool heard the voice of Jellycoe Jack cutting through the swirling wind like a knife.

"Stir yourselves you puny prawns!" he yelled over the din of the screeching wind. Never mind your sleeping, there's a truly devilish tempest up 'ere now. Hurry up you slothful slugs. Last one on deck will suck my socks clean!"

A huge wave swept over the side of the ship and the crest of it poured over the gunwale into the gun deck, washing overboard both a cannon and an unlucky pirate who had been frantically trying to close one of the gun ports that had been wrenched open by the force of the water lashing the Mardy Meg on all sides.

That night the storm worsened; waves drew themselves up into vast walls of water and the wind tore at the ship relentlessly, pushing the Mardy Meg this way and that, like a cat playing with a mouse.

Jellycoe Jack looked out through the porthole. "Work harder, and faster than the slimy snails you are! We's a-getting very close to the shore" he warned, "They say that drowning is a horrible way to die but it's no more than a gaggle of greasy grapefruits like you deserve!". He pushed a couple of terrified pirates out onto the deck with express orders to steer the ship away from the rocky shore.

The wind shrieked and a sickening scraping noise told the pirates their worst nightmare had come true. The Mardy Meg had become stuck on the rocks.

"Abandon ship, abandon ship!" yelled Jellycoe Jack. "Every pirate for himself!"

There was a flurry of activity as the pirates on deck began to panic and look for a way of saving themselves. Jack grabbed the nearest pirate. It was The Admiral. He had collected his concertina and was looking for Cool before finding a way of escaping to the safety of the shore when he felt the sharp tip of Jack's dagger in his back.

"You!" he yelled. "Help me untie my boat and set it over the side," he indicated the only vessel that could be used as a lifeboat, stowed inside the door to his cabin.

With a lot of pulling and heaving and staggering around in the powerful storm, the two men lifted the tiny rowing boat and slowly lowered it overboard. The Admiral placed his bag into the boat, containing his few belongings, including his precious concertina. He had it well wrapped up but didn't want to lose it. He turned to go and find Cool.

"Where are ye going?" Jellycoe Jack roared through the screeching gale. He grabbed The Admiral by the arm. "Get in; I will need more than one pair of hands to row to safety. Get in I say!"

As they climbed into the rowing boat and frantically pulled on the oars a tower of water hit the Mardy Meg and with a terrible creak she slipped off the rocks and into the bubbling sea.

Chapter 5

Retishella sat on the storm-making rock and sang an angry song. Her hair and eyes were hopelessly muddy brown. Still she was not completely powerless and every time she sang high the waves grew stronger. Some times she sang low and threatening, making the wind more powerful than before. She had been sitting here, singing for hours and hours, pouring out her feelings of anger and sorrow into a song that guided the wind and the sea. Just as the fiery orange of the winter sun backlit the clouds on the horizon before starting its nightly journey under the sea, she noticed the Mardy Meg, helplessly tossing up and down on the sea-saw waves at the entrance to the bay. Things started to make sense to her.

"What was it Mersia said?" she wondered out loud. "A landish boy on a boat made from wood and cloth…. This is the only boat made from wood and cloth I have seen today. This must be where my cordella is!"

Skilfully she changed the tone and pitch of her song to gradually push the Mardy Meg on to the rocky shore by the storm-making rock, where it stuck until she reached a note so high it created a towering column of water that crashed down on to the ship and sent it slipping and sliding into the waves.

Just as the last trace of the Mardy Meg disappeared under the bubbling water, and while the pirates were too busy struggling to the rocky shore to notice a mermaid, she slipped off the storm-making rock. As soon as she stopped singing, the storm began to calm down, allowing her to swim quickly over to the wreck of the Mardy Meg and start searching the sinking ship. There was only one landish person left inside, the boy she had seen the day she lost her cordella. He was struggling to free himself from ropes that tied him to the furniture, desperate to get off the ship as it was rapidly filling with water, but he stopped for a moment when he caught sight of Retishella, her hair and eyes shining despite their muddy brown colour. She held out her hand and even though she didn't say anything, Cool knew what she wanted. He put his hand in first one pocket then the other and Retishella saw the look on his face turn to puzzled panic. He shrugged his shoulders and shook his head.

By this time the water had reached his neck, and Retishella realised that the boy would not live very long under the water. She sang the dream spell that had worked so well on the beach earlier that day, and when his eyes had turned dreamy blue she untied him, before dragging his lifeless body out of the sinking ship and laying him on a flat rock on the shore. She remembered Mersia's instruction about the green stone and slipped it into his trouser pocket.

"When you find this stone you must return my cordella to me," she whispered into his ear, hoping he would understand and help her, before turning to keep watch from behind the storm-making rock.

Chapter 6

Cool woke on the shore by the rocks the following morning feeling lucky to be alive. He didn't remember much about how he came to free himself from the ropes and reach safety, but he guessed that his struggles must have worked and he reasoned that he had somehow been washed up by the tide. He looked around to see if anyone else had survived the great storm. Over by the cliff was a jumbled huddle of soggy pirates clustered around a driftwood fire.

Cool recalled a strange dream about a mermaid and a comb. He felt in his pocket and then remembered that he no longer had the comb. He looked across to where Ghastly was deep in conversation with a couple of pirates, jabbing a finger close to their faces to make his point. As he studied Ghastly's face to try and make out what he was saying, he heard the same moaning sound that surrounded the ship last night. Ghastly winced and put his hand in the pocket where Cool had seen him stash the comb. Cool turned with a smile to look out over the mounds of grey sea lashing the large rock on the shore. It was the place where he thought he had seen the mermaid.

"Still scratching at him aren't you?" he smirked and then stopped in his tracks. He swore he could see a pair of eyes watching them from behind the screens of seaweed that smothered the rock. He remembered the beauty of the muddy brown eyes from somewhere. The clear gaze that seemed to look right into his heart and thoughts.

"The mermaid!" he exclaimed under his breath. "It must have been her that saved me last night when the ship was going down. It's the same one, I'm sure of it."

Suddenly Cool realised something shocking.

"The mermaid needs that comb. It is somehow very important to her. Important enough to sink a ship and chase after the people on it."

He looked back towards the rock where he had last glimpsed the mermaid watching them from behind the seaweed. He couldn't see her but he thought he heard an angry, shrieking song coming from the rock, muffled by the blustery wind.

"Last night she thought I had the comb" continued Cool to himself, "because she had seen me pick it up. She doesn't know Ghastly has it."

He took one last look out over the sea. The mermaid was well hidden. But he knew she was there.

As he reached the clump of shivering pirates, Cool heard Jellycoe Jack's voice booming out orders.

"You!" he said, indicating a group of pirates huddled together for warmth. "We needs to find the large green rock in the shape of a pyramid. Find it for me and I won't have you flogged, you hopeless hairballs."

"Will he never give in?" muttered one of the pirates as they tramped sullenly past Cool. "We nearly died last night, we have no ship and he's acting like nothing happened." They disappeared into a thick forest of dead and dying trees on the eastern edge of the beach, still moaning to each other.

Jellycoe Jack turned to the rest of the assembled pirates and cracked his whip to get their attention.

"You, moaning mess of mildew! You must find us something to eat on this godforsaken island. We lost all our food rations in the storm. Go now, and don't you dare to come back empty handed." He cracked his whip again and Cool joined the scattering pirates on their quest for food.

As they climbed the rocky hill out of the bay the sight that met their eyes was not promising. They could see right across the island to the far shore.

"Not very big, is it?" said one of the pirates.

"Can't be more than a couple of miles square, give or take," replied another.

"Where are we going to find food here?" asked a third pirate, surveying the island with dismay.

A dismal sight it was indeed. Beside the long, thin forest of mostly dead trees, a twisted jumble of dry wood that bordered the wind-lashed east of the island, the rest of the land consisted of boggy marsh that hugged and smothered the ground like a wet blanket. The pirates decided to search around the edge of the island for food.

The sandy beaches that encircled the island were beautiful. Each one of the perfect crescent bays was sheltered by rocky hills and cliffs. Bright white sand stretched from the rocks out to the shore and was studded with shells like jewels on a crown. Seaweed draped over rock pools, swaying emerald green in the salty water. The pirates foraged in the clear rock pools and collected a few shellfish and a couple of crabs foolhardy enough to be out in the wintry chill, but knew it wouldn't be enough. They felt happier though, when they came across a crystal clear waterfall, water pure enough to drink tossed from the top of a cliff on to the beach below. Cool stood in the refreshing shower of cold water, washing the sand and dirt of the previous night out of his clothes and body.

When he took off his wet trousers and spread them on the beach to dry in the fierce wind, something fell out of his pocket. It was a green stone, pointed at the top, with blunt barbs of stone carved out of the bottom that looked like they slotted into something. On the side was a carving of a rock and letters that made up the word PYRAMID.

Cool stood for a while, waiting for his clothes to dry, studying the strange stone, and wondering how it came to be in his pocket.

"It must mean something," he said to himself. "It can't be a coincidence that it is carved with the word pyramid."

He was still thinking about it as he dried himself as best he could with a handful of shrivelled up seaweed and pulled on his damp clothes. It wasn't long before the other pirates came over to join him and he quickly stashed the stone in his back pocket.

The rest of the morning was spent finding wood suitable to carve into makeshift water carriers. When they arrived back at the cliff overlooking the bay, they met up with Ghastly standing staring out to sea. He turned abruptly when he heard them coming. Cool wondered if he knew about the mermaid.

"Found any food?" Ghastly asked, standing directly in their way.

"This is a barren place, Sir," one of the pirates started to explain. A solid cuff around the head was his only answer but it did give them time to rush past Ghastly and half run, half slide down into the bay, where they were met with looks of hungry misery.

Jellycoe Jack threw back the tattered curtain he had draped over half a dozen planks of wood to make a shelter. He stood in the doorway like a prince in a palace.

"I told ye not to return without food!" he yelled, hunger swelling his temper.

"But Sir," explained Cool. "This island is a dead place, only dying trees and treacherous bogs as far as the eye can see. The only living place is the beach and we did manage to trap a few shellfish and some crabs."

Jellycoe Jack lifted his whip to lash out at Cool, but one of the other pirates interrupted.

"We do have drinking water. Clean, pure, cold out of the ground. Here, Captain, Sir, please drink!"

Jellycoe Jack stopped in his tracks and picked up one of the wooden water carriers before drinking deeply. They had not found anything to drink among the floating litter, beaching itself from the wreck of the Mardy Meg. The other pirates watched, licking their lips in anticipation.

"It is true, we have water!" Jellycoe Jack announced. "Drink, everyone and be grateful you have such a bountiful captain as can supply you with fresh drinking water in such a bleak place."

The pirates dutifully thanked Jellycoe Jack, and sang his praises while they passed around the drinking water. Jellycoe Jack pocketed the shellfish and crabs and retired to his living quarters.

Some of the pirates fashioned fishing rods out of bits of seaweed tied to stick and sat on the edge of the rocks, dipping them into the water. They didn't look very hopeful but they felt they had to do something. Cool took himself off to sit in peace and quiet of the other end of the bay. He pulled the stone from his pocket and turned it around and about in his hands, studying the inscription.

"I'm looking for a rock in the shape of a pyramid," he reasoned to himself, "and here in my pocket is a carving of a rock and the word PYRAMID. I wish I could work it out."

He gazed out across the fizzing tide, his eyes searching for a glimpse of shiny brown eyes or a flicker of a tail, his thoughts deep and puzzled.

Chapter 7

Retishella peered from behind the storm-making rock at the pirates gathered on the shore. She realised that the boy no longer had her comb, but needed to know if one of the others did.

She sighed a long, deep moan and the wind hustled up the beach. She watched carefully to see if any of the pirates were stung by the teeth on her comb, but couldn't tell.

She tried several more sounds, high shrieks, loud bawls, guttural snarls. Each time she examined the reactions of the pirates on the beach. Eventually, by the twitches and pained looks of one of the group, she narrowed it down to Ghastly.

"It's him," she said to herself. "The tall, angry one that is so cruel to the others. He has my comb."

She howled long and pitiful and saw Ghastly jump and adjust something in his pocket.

Yes, it's definitely him she thought. But how to get it back off him? That was going to be difficult.

She needed to find a way to contact the boy, to make him see the seriousness of her problem. Maybe he would help her.

She noticed several of the pirates were crouched on the rocks in the turning tide trying to catch fish with bits of seaweed tied to the end of sticks.

"That'll never work," she told herself. "The fish around here aren't so stupid as to fall for that trick."

Retishella knew the reputation of Obscurity Island for being a bleak, barren place where very little grew and few creatures wanted to live.

"Perhaps if I help them by giving them some food, they'll feel like helping me in return," she reasoned hopefully.

Retishella returned to the outskirts of her village where she knew her clan would leave food for her until she found her cordella and could return to them. They were bending the rules leaving her food, but she knew them well enough to expect them to do all they could to help her.

Sure enough, a feast of crunchy breakwaterweed pies, thick colisca stew and hot bluerock juice had been packed up in a rock box marked with the village name.

She took out all the breakwaterweed pies and swam back to the island.

The pirates were still fishing when she reached the island, but they hadn't had any luck in catching anything.

She heard them talk to each other and clutch at their empty bellies. She realised they were starving.

She grabbed a patch of green weed from the storm-making rock and used it to camouflage her as she swam under their fishing lines, tying a breakwaterweed pie to each one. Then she hid behind the storm-making rock and watched expectantly.

The pirates pulled the green Breakwaterweed pies out of the water. She saw them untie the pies from the end of their fishing lines and chuck them aside with displeasure.

"Stupid humans," she said to herself. "They don't recognise good food when they see it."

The boy was sitting further along the beach by the rocks, studying Mersia's stone. Retishella picked up a breakwaterweed pie and swam over to him, getting as close as she could in the shallows around the rocks.

The boy was so occupied by the puzzle of Mersia's stone that he didn't notice Retishella until she poked her head out of the water and called to him.

"Hey you, boy," she called although she knew he couldn't understand her.

He looked up and smiled at her. He began walking over to her babbling something in his language and pointing to the pirate she had guessed had her cordella. She realised he was trying to tell her about it. She put up a hand to silence him and held up a breakwaterweed pie. She took a little nibble and then offered it to the boy, smiling and nodding her head to encourage him to try a piece.

He took a small bite, and a flood of savoury, buttery flavours hit his tongue. It was the most delicious thing he had tasted for a long time. He took a larger bite and when Retishella motioned for him to eat it all he gulped it down in one go.

He said something to her that she guessed must be thanks and flashed her his brightest smile.

Retishella pointed to the pirates on the rocks on the far side of the bay, their fishing lines still in the water, piles of breakwaterweed pies at their side. Then she disappeared under the waves to watch from a safe distance.

Sure enough, the boy went over to the pirates and persuaded them that the crunchy, green weed that they had pulled from the sea was edible. She saw them examining the pies, sniffing them and finally taking a taste before scoffing the lot and looking over the rocks for more.

Retishella felt like she had just done something generous and it made her feel good, like she was needed by someone. She decided she would bring some more food for them later.

Chapter 8

Cool looked across at the rock where he knew the mermaid was hiding. He needed to find her and thank her for her kindness in feeding them all. He wanted her to know that he would help her get her comb back, that he realised it was important to her.

The tide was coming in steadily, gradually covering the rock in the middle of the bay, but Cool reckoned it would only come up to his knees at the moment. He took off his shoes and launched himself, fully-clothed into the chill of the rolling waves.

When he reached the rock and searched through the emerald swathes of seaweed that covered it, he realised the mermaid was gone. He climbed up on to the ledge he had seen her sit on earlier that day and stared out to sea, in the hope of seeing her. The top of the rock was jagged and blunt as if a piece had broken off the tip. As he clung to it to get a better view, he realised it was slightly hollow and marked with square holes, evenly spaced. He climbed up to have a closer look and with a thrill of excitement wondered if the stone in his pocket might fit into the hollow.

He lifted the stone to his face and studied the inscription. The main body of the rock he was standing on did indeed look like the picture carved on the stone, except that the picture on the stone reached out of the waves and sloped to a sharp point. He looked back up at the rock. It was definitely the same one, but something was wrong, it seemed somehow unfinished.

With the incoming tide beginning to swirl around his thighs, he slotted the stone into the hollow at the top of the rock. Hardly daring to breathe he heard it click into place. The rock began to shake, a stony tremble that fanned out in the water around him like the wake of a pebble in a pond. A low rumbling on the shore and a grating, scraping sound from the beach sent a flurry of alarm and panic among the pirates. Cool clung to the quivering rock and looked across to the spot where the pirates were all gathered at one end of the beach, calling excitedly to Jellycoe Jack. Something had turned their hungry lethargy into fearful wonder.

By the time Cool waded back to shore, the pirates, including Jellycoe Jack were crowded together staring into a cavern that had appeared in the rose-coloured cliffs by the rocky outcrop they had fished from earlier on.

The cavern entrance was tall and thin, running from the ground to high above their heads in the cliff, just wide enough for one person at a time. Inside a passageway sloped steeply down into smothering blackness that caused a prickle of apprehension among all those looking into it.

Jellycoe Jack held a hapless pirate by the ear and was pushing him in the direction of the cavern. He snarled into the ear he pinched between his bony fingers.

"You! Gibbering jellyfish, get in there and don't come out until you find something. And consider it an honour to be serving your captain, even if you die trying."

The pirate was wincing and moaning with pain, but was more scared of Jellycoe Jack than anything that might be lying in wait for him in the cavern. Shaking himself free of Jack's pincer grip, he stopped only to light a stick of wood from the fire before launching himself into the darkness.

The whole crew assembled on the beach holding their breath, muttering among themselves while they waited. For a while there was nothing, and then the pirate emerged, leaping into the late afternoon light, bedraggled and wild-eyed.

"Tis true! Tis true!" he called over and over, until Jack caught him by the hand and slapped his face.

"Calm 'ee down man, and tell me what is in there," he ordered.

The pirate rubbed his red cheek.

"In there…." He said breathlessly, "gold, jewels, silver, coin, piles and piles of it. So much treasure!"

Jellycoe Jack's eyes bulged with greed. He pushed roughly past the confused pirate, grabbed his lighted torch from him and rushed in to the cavern. The pirates gave a huge cheer and after hurriedly lighting torches themselves, followed Jack into the murky blackness of the cavern.

Cool grabbed a lighted torch and turned to give it to The Admiral, who shook his head.

"You go Cool," he said, "I expect it'll be a disappointment again. Anyway, I want to keep an eye on Ghastly. He's still up there on top of the cliff looking out to sea, with all this excitement going on below. Tis not natural."

Cool nodded and smiled at The Admiral. Then he turned and followed the others into the cavern.

Inside the narrow passageway carved out of solid rock the path sloped steeply down into an underground chamber deep below the surface of Obscurity Island. It was a vast, roughly-hewn circular space and at one end, scooped out of the rock like a stage or platform was a deep shelf that twinkled and glittered in the torchlight as they approached it.

A long, deep sigh of pleasure came from Jellycoe Jack's mouth as he surveyed the wonderful sight before him. Golden coins were strewn across the shelf like confetti at a wedding, ingots piled up like towers of gold, rubies and diamonds oozed out of boxes and chests. Jack fell to his knees, giving thanks to a God that he hadn't spoken to for years.

But as Jack leant forward to pick up a diamond brooch that lay close to the edge of the shelf, his hand was stopped by an invisible barrier.

"My treasure!" he wailed and laid the flat of his hand against the barrier, following it up and down and around. "My lovely treasure is locked behind a sheet of glass!" He pressed himself up against the glass and stared longingly at the treasure. Then he turned and ordered the pirates.

"Quick, you lolloping lumps of lard, help me break it."

The pirates picked up rocks and started hurling them at the glass, but their rocks made little impression. Their swords and daggers were no better.

"Stand back!" called a pirate with a gun and he fired from close range directly at the glass barrier. It barely scratched the surface.

"It is indeed a very thick and strong piece of glass," said one of the pirates who had been examining the effects of the bullet. "It may even be bewitched. It will not be easily broken."

Jellycoe Jack lashed out at the pirate. That was not what he wanted to hear.

"Now what do we do?" he moaned, "Come on you disgraceful dumbo, think!"

One of the pirates standing at the side of the shelf called out "Captain, there are carvings on the wall here, come and see, what do you think they mean?"

The throng of pirates parted to let Jellycoe Jack through. He looked closely at the carvings cut into the rocky wall.

"Four different symbols," he called. "A tree, an acorn, a heart and a ship. It must be a clue to opening the chamber of treasure."

He reached out a finger to trace the outline of the carved ship. As he did there was a grating sound and the ship carving sank into the wall. Behind the sheet of glass with a crash and a tinkle, part of the shelf gave way and some of the treasure disappeared out of view into the vast darkness of the cavern.

"No! What trickery is this? The treasure, where is it gone?" called Jellycoe Jack, lashing out at nearby pirates even though it was his fault some of the treasure had disappeared. He pressed his face up against the glass barrier and tried to see what had happened to it. "Tis not there!" he moaned, "So much gold and jewels, snuffed out in the twinklin' of an eye."

The pirates stood around watching in astonishment as Jellycoe Jack wiped a tear from his eye and blew his nose on his sleeve.

"Move back, clumsy clutsoes," he ordered. "No one touch anything until we work this out. We can't lose any more treasure."

The pirates all huddled together in the middle of the cavern away from the walls.

"Now then," he continued, more to himself than the others. "Those symbols must mean something. If we could work it out we could solve the puzzle that has been set for us here." He tapped himself on the forehead and paced up and down, the pirates following him. "Think, Jack, Think!"

"Where did you get the original map?" asked Cool.

"What do you mean, lad?" Jellycoe Jack moved closer to Cool and grabbed him by his coat collar.

"Well," continued Cool, trying not to be intimidated by Jack, "if you remember it might give us a clue."

"True enough," replied Jack, releasing Cool from his grip. "But the map came to me in a roundabout way. It could've been drawn up by any one of many pirates, now all dead."

"But where did you get it from?" Cool persisted.

"Garston Bones gave it to me. Said he found it clutched in the dead hands of Johnny Jenks, captain of the Rosa Mundi when we defeated her, shortly before you joined us."

There was a flutter of muttering from the pirates about how it had been a terrible battle, with the loss of several brave pirates and great damage to the Mardy Meg. It was the reason they had put into port in Cool's hometown, to repair and restock the ship.

"Garston, tell us again, what happened when you found the map," Jack called over the heads of the pirates.

"He's not here," called one of the pirates from the back of the crowd. "He must have stayed behind on the beach."

"Keeping guard, yes, keeping guard," Jack said, with an edge of doubt in his voice.

"I keeps the map in my pocket for safety," he continued, pulling a wadge of folded tatty brown paper from his pocket.

"It may help solve the mystery if we look at it again," Cool suggested helpfully, getting ready to duck if the captain lashed out.

Jellycoe Jack unfolded the paper.

"Here, boy, bring that torch closer, tis hard to see anything in this gloom."

Cool held up his torch and studied the map over the captain's shoulder.

"See, here is the island mapped out with the dying forest and the peaty bog." Jellycoe Jack indicated with a blackened fingernail. "Here are the sandy beaches, and at the bottom is an inscription describing a 'normous green rock in the shape of a pyramid. All those things we already know. I see no further clues, nothing to tell us how to solve the puzzle we see before us."

"What about the other side?" Cool said.

Jack flipped the map over.

"Tis nothing but lines and dots on the other side, a code the likes of which I never saw before."

"But I've seen it before," Cool announced with rising excitement. "It is music written down, The Admiral told me."

"And can he understand this music written down?" asked Jack.

"Yes, he played me a tune from some music written down. It must be a clue or else why would it appear here on the map?"

"Where is The Admiral?" asked Jack. "Bring him and his squeeze box to me at once."

Cool nodded and ran with his torch spluttering along the narrow passageway out of the cavern and on to the beach. The afternoon sun was hidden behind clouds, but still gave out enough light to blur his vision for a moment after the darkness of the cavern. The Admiral was still staring up at Ghastly, who tended a bonfire on the top of the rocky hill.

"Admiral, Admiral it is true! We have found great treasure in this cave. But we cannot reach it until a mystery is solved. A puzzle written in music. You are to come with me at once and play it on your concertina."

"I've been watching him," The Admiral said, indicating Ghastly. "He's up to something."

They climbed up the rocks by the side of the cavern until they reached a nook like a little shelf where The Admiral had put his concertina for safekeeping, out of the way of the weather and the tide. The shelf was just under the feet of Ghastly hidden from his view by an overhang of rock, but they could see the smoke from the fire above whipping up in the freshening wind.

The Admiral looked out over the bay and grabbed Cool by the arm, pointing to the flat blue of the horizon out at sea.

"So, that's your game Garson Bones. The fire is a beacon," he muttered under his breath.

Cool looked in the direction of The Admiral's pointing finger. "Oh, yes, I see it," he replied in a shocked whisper. "I can just make out the tops of four masts. She must be a sizeable ship."

"Can't quite make out the flag she's flying yet. But how did Ghastly know she was there?"

"Come," said Cool, remembering why he had been sent to The Admiral. "We need to get back to the captain and get the treasure. It'll be a while till that ship gets here. We must tell the captain and work out what to do."

They climbed down the rocks in silence, each deep in thought.

When they arrived in the cavern, Jellycoe Jack was still studying the map for clues.

"Captain, I have something important to tell you," said The Admiral.

"In a moment, in a moment," Jack dismissed his news with a wave of his hand. "Nothing is more important than this treasure. Have ye got your instuurment?"

"Yes, Captain, but I really must…"

"Desist dungbreath!" Jack lashed out with his hand and caught The Admiral across the cheek. "I needs to think." He showed The Admiral the music. "Do you know this?"

"Yes, it looks like the tune you gave me on that paper you found in a trunk. Cool here says he recognises it as a song. A Navy man's song, not a pirate one. He started to play.

It was indeed the tune for Hearts of Oak. As The Admiral played, a screeching sound came from the sheet of glass that trapped the treasure. Then it started to move, like a window winding down into the ground beneath them.

"It's working, the booootiful bowowowntiful treasure will soon be all mine, all mine!" Jack called excitedly. He looked around and added nervously, "I mean, all ours, all ours!"

When The Admiral reached the end of the tune he stopped. The barrier stopped moving.

"Keep playing, don't stop if you know what's good for you," Jack cuffed the back of the Admiral's head.

"Keep playing tills we can reach the treasure."

The Admiral started to play again. But the barrier didn't move. He tried again, but nothing happened.

"Play louder, play faster," ranted Jack. "Do something; only let the glass move further."

The Admiral played the song faster and louder with no success. Jack was frantically trying to climb the wall of glass to get to the narrow opening in the top made by The Admiral's music. He finally slid down and sat in a crumpled heap on the floor of the cave, staring gloomily through the glass at the treasure while The Admiral continued to play the tune.

When The Admiral reached the chorus Cool started to sing the words his mother had taught him.

"Hearts of oak are our ships…."

With a whining scrape the barrier started moving again. Jellicoe Jack stood back from the sheet of glass and joined in singing with Cool.

"Don't just sit there with your mouths open like hoards of hapless haddock, sing!"

There was a cheer from the pirates, who all started to join in with the chorus and kept singing as the barrier steadily lowered. The loudest singing voice of all belonged to Jellicoe Jack.

Chapter 9

The sound of many voices singing and a strange instrument playing a tune caught Retishella's ear and she peered from behind the rocks towards the sandy beach. When she saw the opening to the cavern she stared in wide-eyed excitement.

"So it is true!" she whispered to herself. "I had heard stories of the great Clandestine Cave on this island and of the many brave merpeople who had risked their lives to find it."

She remembered the words of a song her aunt Marla, a great singer and storyteller, used to sing when she told stories of the Clandestine Cave:

In Secret's Cave a treasure lies
Deep in Obscurity
But only can the good and wise
Know what it really means.

A scuffing noise from above her and a shower of rocks and sand made her look up. The other pirate, the one with her cordella was climbing down the cliff on to the beach. He was too far away for her to reach out and grab him, so she hid herself behind the rocks and watched with great interest, waiting for a chance to take her cordella back and return to her family.

The pirate stood by the entrance to the Clandestine Cave, examining it carefully. Retishella expected him to go in after the pirates, but instead he turned and waded through the tide to the storm-making rock. The water by now was waist high and only the top of the rock was above the water, but the pirate was determined to reach it.

"Now's my chance!" she thought to herself. "If I can just drag him off the rock …"

Before she had a chance to think, the pirate had reached the storm-making rock and was climbing up it. When he got to the tip of the rock he took off the stone, the one the boy had placed on top of it earlier. The whole bay shook again, as if hit by an earthquake and with a scraping, groan the entrance to the Clandestine Cave started to close.

Retishella could see a glint of gold from his ghoulish grin as the pirate looked at the stone in his hand and then back at the cave and laughed as he watched the entrance close.

The pirate shouted something in a triumphant voice and then cackled wildly like a madman.

Retishella shivered. How could he be so callous? The pirates were trapped in the cave. They would never find a way out.

She swam over to him, singing the dream song. The pirate stopped for a moment, his eyes beginning to glaze over as she sang. A pinch from the cordella in his pocket brought him round and he shook off the effect of her song. Without her cordella Retishella's song was not as powerful as normal.

The pirate climbed from the storm-making rock and started wading in the water to the shore. Retishella seized her chance and launched herself at him. He pushed on for the shore as she grabbed hold of one of his legs and pulled for all she was worth. If she could only get him under the water she would be able to get her cordella back.

The pirate stopped wading. By now the water came to just above his knees. Retishella wrapped her hands around his right knee as tightly as she could. The pirate lifted his other foot out of the water and with a sickening thud it slammed down on Retishella's head. She felt dizzy, but she knew she had to get away before things got worse. She turned tail and dived with all her might, just making it as far as the bottom of the storm-making rock before everything went black.

Chapter 10

Jellycoe Jack sat in the cavern surrounded by treasure. He had a smile of intense pleasure on his lips, and was gurgling like a contented baby. Cool thought he looked hideous, but at least he had stopped hurling abuse and whipping people.

The pirates were busy gathering up as much of the hoard as they could when the ground all around them started to shake and they heard the terrifying sound of the cavern door closing. Cool and the pirates ran towards the cavern door, just in time to see the last thin slice of daylight disappear and leave them staring at each other in stunned silence by the flickering light of the torches.

"We's all trapped!" one of the pirates shouted. They started running about in panic calling out their horror and fear.

Cool ran back to Jellycoe Jack.

"Captain, the door is closed, we are trapped. Do you know of another way out?"

Jack just looked at him and smiled. "My treasure!" he muttered, "Isn't it lovely?"

"But Captain," several of the pirates joined Cool by now. "We cannot get out. The entrance is closed. What are we to do?"

"My lovely treasure…" whispered Jack, a dreamy expression on his face.

"Listen Captain," continued Cool, "what use is your treasure to you if you cannot get out of here? You cannot eat gold. Diamonds will not open the door back out into the daylight."

Jack snuggled down into his pile of gold with a deep sigh of pleasure.

"He's not able to help us at the moment," Cool announced to the pirates nearest to him. He stood on a rock to be better heard and called all the pirates to attention.

"The captain is taken sick. We must find a way out. We must do it without panic and we must be methodical."

He directed groups of pirates to various parts of the cavern. They disappeared into the darkness amid cries of 'good luck', 'safe return' and 'be careful'.

"Cool," called The Admiral, "Come here."

Cool crawled into a low, uneven passageway, ducking and stooping to avoid a maze of overhanging lumps and bumps on the ceiling. His feet stumbled and slipped on the damp, rocky ground. At the end of the passageway was another cave, a great wide expanse of rock with a low roof. If he stood with his neck sunk into his shoulders he could just about stand up in it. It felt cooler in here, with water dripping down the walls, leaving a trail of crystal in their wake. At the far end of the cave, stretching from one side to another was a lake of water, a lagoon. Cool turned at the sound of The Admiral, huffing and puffing as he wrenched his broad body out of the narrow passageway and into the cave.

"I thought you said you had found something," said Cool.

"I have," replied The Admiral, half walking, half crawling over to the lagoon. He dipped his hand in the water and scooped up a sip. "Taste this water, it is salt."

"And?"

"If it is salt it must be seawater. That means it comes in from the sea outside. What gets in can also get out."

Cool stared long and hard at the lagoon.

"Yes!" he remarked, "you are right. And if we could follow the lagoon we would end up outside the cave."

He looked at The Admiral and realised they had both just thought of the only drawback to this plan.

"We would have to be able to swim underwater," said Cool.

"And we don't know how long for," added The Admiral.

They both sat, dejectedly staring at the only points of light in the thick darkness, two circles of flickering torchlight, reflecting turquoise in the water.

Chapter 11

Retishella's head hurt. She had a bump the size of a seagull's egg on the back of her head and her eyes were seeing double.

"The pirate with my cordella," she remembered, rubbing her head. "Where did he go?"

She clung on to the storm-making rock and gradually inched her way up, eventually flopping exhausted on to a ledge. She felt weak and wanted to be sick.

She took several deep breaths to help her focus on her surroundings. The sight before her eyes was more sobering than any medicine.

Anchored off the entrance to the bay was a huge ship of wood and cloth, much bigger than the pirate ship she had wrecked. She dropped down into the water again, fear pumping strength back into her body.

The beach opening to the Clandestine Cave was still blocked by rock, and Retishella remembered that the pirates were trapped inside. All except for one. The one that had her cordella. She looked to the shore, her eyes tracking the scattering of rocks that outlined the bay, and then she saw him. He was on the beach staring through a long looking glass out at the ship. He was too far on land to be reached.

"If he goes on that ship I may never get my cordella back!" Retishella realised with a shiver.

"I must stop him."

She thought for a moment, looking from the ship to the pirate on the shore and then to the closed Clandestine Cave. There had to be a solution here somewhere.

"If I release the pirates they will not be happy with the one who shut them in the cave," she reasoned. "In the confusion I could get my cordella back. Or I could ask the friendly boy to help me; he seems to have more understanding than most of these wicked landish pirates."

She searched her memory for stories she had been told about the Clandestine Cave. There was an underwater entrance by the shore. She guessed it must be near the beach entrance, over among the rocks the pirates had fished on earlier. She stopped to calm herself and focus on the task ahead, and then she ducked her head under the foaming sea and swam towards the rocks.

Finding the underwater entrance was not difficult and soon Retishella was staring into the opening of a long, dark tunnel sloping up into the rock. But she was afraid. Afraid of the stories. The stories of the Cheerless Witch.

The reason no one knew much about the Clandestine Cave was because no one had ever managed to get past the witch. Many brave souls tried, armed with a variety of weapons from stun jelly fish to charms and spells. But the witch had always managed to outwit them. People said she killed them then ate them.

Retishella looked up into the complete blackness of the tunnel. She realised she had little other choice.

"I must make it as easy for myself as I can. I will need a light to find my way through the dark. I have no strength to fight and do not have any weapons. I must find my own way of defeating the Cheerless Witch."

She knew of a ready source of glowfish in glass jars. It would mean a secret visit to her home village. If she was seen it would have disastrous consequences for herself and her whole family. But she could think of no other way.

Chapter 12

Cool and The Admiral sat in the chill of the lagoon cave, the only sound the lapping of the water against the rocky walls. Their thoughts seemed to shout around their heads among the quiet shadows. They had to find a way out.

"What do you think Ghastly was up to?" asked Cool.

"Treachery of some kind, no doubt." The Admiral didn't hide the anger in his voice.

"Do you think it was all a plan, to entice us here and then trap us in this cave?"

"Could be so, lad. But what I'm puzzled over is why did he leave us in here with the treasure?"

"Maybe one of the others will know something. The Captain is in no state to listen."

"Gold fever, I've seen it before." The Admiral stared into the blackness and took a deep breath. "Some times the wanting for gold is so great, it takes over a man's life and soul. When he finally finds the gold it drives him out of his senses."

"Do you think he will recover?"

"Aye lad, there is a cure. It involves getting him away from the gold."

"But that won't be easy, Admiral, will it? Not in his present state of mind."

"No lad. It won't be easy, but it is the only way for our poor foolish captain. Let's go and tell the others what we know. Maybe if we pool our knowledge we can put the pieces of this puzzle together and find a solution."

Chapter 13

Retishella slowed to a quiet glide as she reached her home village. It looked different, deserted. Normally at this time of day there would be activity all around; people tending crops and animals; children playing junkball among the rocks; the bustle of cooking, eating, cleaning, living everyday life. But she could see no one. A mournful noise caught her attention and she realised why the village was empty. Many of the grown-ups were gathered in the great cave used for celebrations and ceremonies. She hid in a plagoweed bush and listened. The people of her village were holding vigil for her, singing songs of her speedy and safe return. She wiped away tears of gratitude, thankful that they should care so much about her. She had become used to the way the pirates treated each other and had forgotten how good kindness could feel.

"How proud am I that I am a merperson." The thought washed through her whole body, boosting it with renewed energy.

A loud male solo wafted across to her and sent a tremble of longing down her spine and tail. She recognised the voice as her father.

"Oh father, I wish so dearly to be back here at home again, with my family and my village friends. I miss you all so much."

She stifled a sob and blew her nose on a plagoweed leaf.

A movement inside the cave roused her and she remembered why she was here. She looked around for a glowfish in a glass jar. There was one by the door. Darting as quickly as she could she snatched the glowfish jar and buried herself back into the plagoweed bush just as her father and mother floated slowly through the door. They were comforting each other with hugs and whispered words.

"Mother, Father," Retishella looked fervently at her parents. "I will find a way to return to you. I promise." She blew them a bubble filled with a promise and a kiss and wrapped herself up in plagoweed to float away undetected.

Chapter 14

Cool and The Admiral joined the other pirates back in the Clandestine Cave. The captain was sleeping like a baby on a bed of gold and jewels.

The last of the pirates sent to find another way out returned from their search and joined the rest of the group still gathered in the middle of the cave, sitting in a group on the ground by the light of their torches.

"Things are looking bad my friends," said Cool. "We are shut in these caves with no obvious way out, and the captain suffers from gold fever. What are we to do?"

"I searched to the east. I only got a couple of caves away from here and came to a dead end," one of the pirates called out.

Several other pirates agreed, adding stories of passages blocked by rock falls or too narrow for a body to pass through, even a little one.

"I don't quite understand," said a short pirate with a bushy black beard, "How did the rock become closed? Did we make it close? Cos if we did, I's a-thinking we can open it again."

Cool spoke up. "I opened the rock door with a kind of rock key that slotted in to the top of the boulder in the middle of the bay; you know the green one in the tide. Turns out that was our emerald green pyramid. As I am in here, trapped with you and don't have the rock any more I can only guess we are the victims of treachery." As one the pirates took in a sharp breath and muttered to each other.

"But who?" asked the bearded pirate. "We are all here in this cave. Who could have shut us in?"

"We are not all here in this cave," The Admiral reminded them. "One of us is missing."

The pirates all looked around at each other. There was a short silence and then the word "Ghastly" passed as a whispered echo among the crew.

"Yes," said The Admiral. "I believe Ghastly did this to us. Before I became trapped inside with you I was sitting on the beach watching him. He has built a bonfire on top of the cliff above the bay and was using it as a beacon to guide a sizeable ship to this very spot."

"A ship?" called a young pirate from the back of the crowd. "What ship?"

"Unfortunately I did not have time to make out the details on the ship before the captain called me here to help solve the treasure puzzle with my music. But I did notice it had four masts, which makes it at least twice the size of the Mardy Meg."

There was a flutter of muttering as the pirates discussed the news.

"But that doesn't explain why," continued the young pirate. "Ghastly had a cushy life on the Mardy Meg, why would he want to betray us?"

"We will have to wait for the answer to that one," replied The Admiral. "In the meantime we must find a way out of here before Ghastly opens the cave up again and whatever band of cutthroats and rascals he has lured here attack us like sitting ducks and steal the treasure from under our noses."

"But we've just spent hours trying in vain to find a way out," the bearded pirate reminded them. The others nodded their heads in agreement.

"There is another possibility," called Cool, standing on a rock to see over the heads of the pirates. They stopped talking and listened.

"The Admiral and I have found a lagoon in a cave through this passageway," he pointed behind them. "It is a saltwater lagoon, which means…"

The bearded pirate finished Cool's sentence with relish, "Where salt water can get in it can also get out!" The pirates started congratulating each other.

"Wait!" called Cool, "the only way out is under water. We do not know how far it is. We do not know if it is humanly possible to swim to safety underwater from here."

The pirates took to muttering again as they digested this latest piece of news.

"Let's go and have a look," suggested a young pirate at the back of the crowd. "It's the only ray of hope we have in this dismal place."

The Admiral signalled them to gather around him by the entrance to the lagoon cave. With renewed hope and high spirits the pirates filed through the narrow gap into the lagoon cave.

Chapter 15

When Retishella arrived back at Obscurity Island, the first thing she did was find a hiding place behind the rocks and look out across the beach and the bay.

The ship was a hive of activity. Lights festooned its deck and rigging, giving it a ghostly gleam in the early evening gloom. The sailors were busy lowering a smaller wooden boat into the water. The pirate that had her cordella watched the ship from behind a bonfire he had lit on the cliff top. Retishella wished she understood what was going on. Was he about to sail away from the island with her cordella, and leave the pirates in the cave to die?

She dived silently, holding the glowfish jar in front of her as she turned her mind to the tunnel and the Cheerless Witch.

She entered the tunnel, hesitating at first and then gliding slowly, using all her senses to make out her surroundings by the shadowy light of one glowfish. As far as she could work out, the walls were uneven and rounded to create a tube of rock on a slight upward slope. Deeper into the tunnel the floor was littered with sand, rocks, shells and long white sticks that Retishella realised with a shiver were bones. She looked back the way she had just come. The light at the entrance to the tunnel was a small disc of blue in the distance. There could be no turning back.

As the tunnel turned a sharp left Retishella heard a sound that stopped her in her tracks. The sound of someone searching through a pile of metal and singing a cursing song of the kind that would have made Retishella's mother wash her mouth out with foaming sea spittle.

As she got closer a form began to take shape before her eyes. An elderly mermaid, with wild, straggly hair and a tail missing more than half of its scales was swimming with her tail near the roof, and her head near the ground of the tunnel. Both hair and tail were white, a white so dull it seemed like no colour at all.

Above her was a deep rift, a narrow opening in the roof, as if someone had taken a knife and cut a slice into it. The mermaid was sifting through the sand on the floor of the tunnel, stopping occasionally to lift an object up to her face, her eyes squinting as she took a close look by the light of a glowfish in a jar tied around her neck.

"The Cheerless Witch!" whispered Retishella to herself, "I wonder why she's grubbing around on the floor of the tunnel?" The Witch held something shiny close to her eyes and studied it for a long time. Retishella held her breath and looked around for a chance to get past the witch and find the Clandestine Cave. Retishella inched past the back of the witch, barely daring to breathe. The witch's attention was completely taken by the thing she was studying.

"Keep looking at that shiny thing," Retishella repeated over and over to herself, as if by thinking it she could make it happen.

Without warning the witch threw the thing she was looking at back over her shoulder and it hit Retishella in the eye.

"Ow!" Retishella said, rubbing her sore eye. The witch nearly jumped out of her skin and with a squawk of surprise, swiftly turned and grabbed Retishella roughly by the arm.

"What are you doing here maid?" She shrieked with a voice like a soprano seagull. Retishella tried to free her arm, but the witch just held on tighter, her fingernails digging in to her like claws.

"Why?" replied Retishella, trying to sound brave and in control. "Do you own this place?"

"No, I don't own it," said the witch in a low, creepy voice, pulling Retishella's face close to her own. "I haunt it."

She shoved Retishella down on to the floor of the tunnel.

"Tell me who you are and what you are doing here?" she ordered.

"Why should I?" the words escaped Retishella's lips before she had a chance to regret them.

"Because my maid, if you don't you'll end up like that pile of bones over there. I'm in need of a bit of entertainment."

Retishella looked over at the mound of bones of various kinds of sea creatures. She couldn't see the bones of any merpeople but she imagined there must be some there. The witch cackled a thin laugh.

"Try again, maid. You are too young to end up a pile of bones in a dark tunnel."

Retishella took a deep breath.

"My name is Retishella and I'm trying to free some pirates in the Clandestine Cave that can help me."

"Liar!" spat the witch. "You are a pirate spy aren't you? A mermaid working for pirates. You disgust me."

"No, really, I…" Retishella started but was interrupted by a slap across the face.

"No more lies maid," the witch sneered. "Let's start with an easier question. Where are you from?"

"I'm from the village by the breakwaterweed beds, not far from here."

The witch hesitated for a moment, and took a deep breath before continuing in a hushed voice, "and who is the head of your village?"

"Her name is Glorishell, and she is a great leader. We have a merrow called..."

"Mersia," the witch and Retishella said this last word together.

The looked at each other uneasily, each one wondering what the other one was up to.

"How did you know…?" Retishella started to ask but was interrupted.

"Never mind that, you still haven't told me what brings you to this desolate island. Haven't you heard the stories of the Clandestine Cave?"

"I lost my cordella by the storm-making rock," Retishella started to sob. "A cruel and vicious pirate has it in his pocket and these other pirates are my only chance of getting it back."

The witch studied Retishella's face to try and make up her mind if the girl was telling the truth.

"That would explain your unusual colouring," the witch reasoned out loud. "Have you been shunned from the village yet?"

"Yes," answered Retishella, "but how did you know that?"

"I've seen it happen before, that's all."

"Can I ask you a question?" Retishella asked softly.

"Depends what it is," the witch held Retishella's arm with one hand, and bent down to pick up a ruby ring from the floor of the tunnel with the other.

"Why are you digging about in the sand here? What are you looking for?"

"A particular gold brooch. Red gold and set with bright green shells. It is very precious to me and I must find it."

"And you're sure its here? In this tunnel?"

"No it's not here in this tunnel," the witch pointed above their heads, "It's up there in the Clandestine Cave where a heartless pirate tossed it on to a pile of treasure. That was nearly one hundred years ago.

Sometimes bits of treasure fall from the platform in the cave and I collect them up, hoping one day to find my brooch again. But I never have." She gave a deep, sad sigh.

"You've been here that long?" Retishella's eyes opened wide with wonder. "No wonder your colour is so unusual."

"My colour is unusual for another reason, maid." Retishella gasped and then asked seriously. "The brooch, is it your cordella?"

The witch nodded. Retishella stopped seeing a brutal and merciless enemy and saw instead a vulnerable old mermaid, far from home and without an important part of her.

"Please," begged Retishella gently, "if I help you find your cordella, will you help me get mine back?"

The witch stopped searching through the rubble on the floor and turned to take a good look at Retishella.

"It is such a long time since I spoke my own language to another mermaid, so long since I met another creature of my own kind. I had forgotten how much I missed my people, my home."

The Witch ran her fingers through Retishella's slimy brown hair before giving her a hug.

"Yes, young maid, I will help you. If it stops another mermaid going through the agonies that I have suffered; the loneliness, the wasted life imprisoned here, all my waking thoughts and words swamped by the need to find my cordella. I will help you if you will help me." The witch managed a weak smile as if she was unused to using her smile muscles.

"Is it true?" asked Retishella. "Did you really kill and eat all those merpeople?"

"It is a story, that's all," the witch shrugged her shoulders. "It stops strangers snooping around. I have survived here by eating fish."

"But all those brave merpeople who never returned from the Clandestine Cave," continued Retishella. "What happened to them?"

"The caves are a dark and dangerous maze of tunnels," replied the witch. "It is easy to find a way in, not so easy to find a way out. I know that, I have spent many years exploring them in the hope of finding my cordella."

"The pirates, they are trapped in the caves by the beach entrance. How do we reach them?"

"Are you sure they will help you maid?" The witch gave Retishella a serious look. "I never knew a pirate that wanted to help a mermaid before. They think we will bring them misfortune."

"There is one that will. He is only young, and I think he has worked out that my comb is important to me and wants to return it."

"I hope you are right maid. I have heard dreadful things happen to mermaids caught by pirates. Follow me, I know of a place where we can find them and they can find us. "

She led the way through the maze of tunnels to the lagoon cave, and for the first time Retishella began to understand how a lobster feels when it is caught in a trap.

Chapter 16

Cool and The Admiral sat looking into the clear green depths of the lagoon. They could see no daylight coming from beneath the water, no obvious exit to the outside world. The pirates decided by a show of hands to leave Cool and The Admiral to find out if there was a way out by the underwater lagoon, and they all returned to the treasure cave to keep an eye on the captain.

"That's nice," mused Cool. "Leaving us to do all the work. They've learnt a lot from Jellycoe Jack, that's for sure."

"Don't be so harsh my lad. Not everyone fancies a dip in the water as readily as you."

"You mean, they are pirates and they are afraid of water?"

"Not afraid, just, well, unused to swimming in it."

"Or not able to swim more like."

The Admiral nodded at Cool and turned his attention to the lagoon, dipping a hand in and swishing it around.

"The water is very cold and deep," he said with a shiver. They sat studying the lagoon in silence for a while, each deciding what to do.

"I think I'll have to go into the water and have a search around," mused Cool. "Sitting here isn't going to help us find our way out." He began to take off his jacket.

"Stop, Cool, look!" The Admiral pointed to the water by the left side of the lagoon where bubbles were rising to the surface.

"Admiral, there's a light;" gasped Cool, "A light under the water and it is coming this way."

The Admiral quickly doused their torches in the water and pulled Cool back away from the water's edge.

Two heads rose up from the lagoon, cutting through the surface together. Cool and the Admiral watched in the shifting shadows, stuck to the spot with fear.

"Mermaids!" gasped The Admiral, inching further back from the water's edge.

Cool breathed a sigh of relief and walked towards the mermaids.

"Cool! No boy, don't go near them. Mermaids always bring bad luck."

"It's alright Admiral," replied Cool, sitting and dangling his legs into the water. "The young mermaid is my friend. She'll help me, I know she will."

The Admiral was not convinced and it showed in his face.

"And anyway," continued Cool. "This just proves our idea. If they can get in, we can get out."

"But Cool, there's still the problem of us not being able to breathe under water like they can," said The Admiral.

The mermaid with the missing comb waved at Cool. Then she motioned him to get into the lagoon. Cool pushed himself off the edge of the ledge and into the chill of the sea.

He had been wondering how he could ask a mermaid that didn't speak his language to help him escape underwater. Then a thought came to him and he decided to give it a try.

He took a deep breath, tipped his legs up over his head and dived straight down into the water. He swam to the wall of the lagoon where they had first noticed the bubbles and started to search for anything that might look like a tunnel.

Several times he dived, surfacing for air when he had to, each time going a bit deeper until it got too deep for him to see by the light the mermaids carried.

The mermaids watched him, a look of puzzlement on their faces. Then the younger mermaid followed him down on one of his dives and handed him what looked like a glass jar on a bit of stringy seaweed, with a glowing fish inside, a kind of underwater torch. She pulled him along the wall a little way until they came to a tunnel entrance.

Cool quickly handed the mermaid back the fish jar and swam urgently to the surface to take a breath of air. The mermaid looked around in surprise to find him gone and then swam to join him.

"Admiral," called Cool gulping breaths of air. " I've found the entrance. Now all I need to know is how long it is. Could I swim it without drowning?"

The younger mermaid gestured to Cool to follow her down again. She jumped at the sound of him taking a deep breath, then took his hand and dragged him down to the entrance of the tunnel He took the jar of light from her and shone it in the tunnel. He couldn't see the end, just blackness. The mermaid took his hand and started to guide him into the rocky entrance. Cool

97

pulled away, too afraid to follow her in. He returned to the Admiral and they sat at the water's edge.

"She's gone again," said The Admiral, "what's she up to? Mermaids; I don't trust them."

"Just wait and see Admiral," Cool replied. "She needs us at the moment, and is willing to help."

The mermaid disappeared for a couple of minutes, then returned and dumped something at the water's edge. It was a scrap of torn canvas, a piece of the wreckage of the Mardy Meg.

"Hey Admiral," called Cool, "It's not far. Reckon even you could do it!"

Cool followed the mermaid into the water again and heard her call over to the other mermaid, who joined them. They each took one of Cool's arms and dived with great speed down into the turquoise depths.

Just as they arrived at the entrance to the tunnel there was a mighty crashing sound, followed by bits of treasure scattering all around them. The older mermaid pushed roughly past them both and thrashed frantically around, picking up and examining small bits of treasure. Cool swam into the tunnel and the younger mermaid took hold of his hand.

They heard a shriek behind them and they saw the older mermaid pin a gold brooch on to her seaweed wrap. She began to shine, as if a powerful light had been turned on her, and her hair, eyes, tail, her whole body shimmered a beautiful emerald green. The younger mermaid dropped Cool's hand for a moment, and started to swim towards her mermaid friend. Cool pulled on her tail as she went past and pointed in panic at his mouth and the bubbles already escaping from it. When she spotted the look on Cool's face, she turned to him and grabbing his hand pulled him through the tunnel, thrashing at the seawater with her tail and swimming with him so fast that the whole tunnel slipped past in a blur. Cool blew out the last of the air in his lungs and felt the urgent need to take a breath. He knew he could not breathe water, and clamped his mouth shut so he was not tempted to try, but every part of his body was crying out for fresh air.

Then he saw the sea around them brightening, and he felt the mermaid pulling him upwards towards the surface. As they broke the surface of the water, Cool gulped the evening air, filling his lungs with huge breaths. The mermaid watched him in horror, wondering if he was going to be alright.

After a couple of minutes gasping and coughing, Cool turned to the mermaid and smiled. He took the mermaid's hand in his and looked into her beautiful hazel eyes.

"Thank you, thank you dear, kind mermaid," he wheezed. "You have once again saved me. I will repay you. I will try and get your comb off Ghastly, I promise."

The mermaid said nothing. Cool didn't know if she understood, but he had to say it anyway. She grinned briefly before hurriedly turning tail and swimming off to join her friend in the tunnel.

Chapter 17

Cool climbed out of the water and hid himself behind a couple of rocks near the cavern. He turned to study the scene in the bay. It filled him with dread. The ship at the entrance to the bay was the biggest he had ever seen, most certainly larger than any he had ever sailed on. He had expected it to be a pirate ship, flying the skull and crossbones on the tallest mast, but instead there was a flag with a blue rose, not one he had ever seen or heard of before.

His attention was distracted from the ship by the sound of gunfire, followed by screaming and shouting coming from inside the cavern. He realised that the scraping sound he had heard before he escaped with the mermaid, the one that sent more treasure sinking to the bottom of the lagoon, was the noise of the cavern door being opened up again.

"What is Ghastly up to?" he wondered.

He ducked back down behind the rocks just as the sailors from the ship marched the crew of the Mardy Meg out of the cavern, poking and prodding them with their rifles to get them to move faster, their torches flickering and smoking in the windy darkness of early evening. The Mardy Meg crew stumbled and slipped, unable to walk steadily on the rocky ground with their hands tied behind their backs. Captain Jellycoe Jack followed behind ranting at his captors. His eyes had lost their glazed expression and now his face was fixed into an angry scowl.

"What kind of mindless muppets are ye? Leaving behind all that gold, all that beautiful treasure."

"Get on with you, worthless pirate scoundrel," one of the sailors growled, pushing Jack with the butt of his rifle. "We'll take the treasure, don't you worry. It belongs to us now."

Jellicoe Jack gave a roar like a bear in pain. "Ye will all rot in your beds once I get my hands free. I've defeated more savage foes than you. We are fearsome pirates as does not sink so low as to tie folk up."

As Cool watched, his friends and fellow pirates were marched down the beach towards a series of small rowing boats, where more armed crew from the ship were waiting to row them out and force them to climb on board.

Cool saw The Admiral among the crowd. He stumbled as he passed Cool's hiding place.

"Hey!" he called in a raised whisper, all the time keeping an eye on the ship's crew members.

"Admiral! What's going on?"

The admiral turned to look at Cool, then gave a warning nod of his head. Ghastly was close behind, and would spot him if he tried to talk. Cool ducked back behind the rocks.

The Admiral called to Ghastly, in a voice loud enough for Cool to hear.

"I saw two mermaids in the lagoon Master Bones. They took young Cool, dragged him under the water and I haven't seen him since." He winked in Cool's direction and carried on marching with the rest of the crowd.

"God help him then," replied Ghastly. "Mermaids bring bad luck and tragedy whenever they have contact with humans."

"Not as much bad luck as having contact with you, it seems," Cool thought to himself. Then he realised something more disturbing. Ghastly was the only pirate from the Mardy Meg that did not have his hands tied behind his back.

"The Admiral was right," he thought with a shock, "Ghastly was out to capture us all along. He is one of them, and we thought he was one of us."

He could do no more than watch as the only people on the island were sailed out to the ship and forced to climb the rope ladders hanging down the sides. He saw them being pushed one behind the other below deck, heavily guarded by uniformed crew armed with guns and swords. His mind raced, searching for a good idea.

Chapter 18

When Retishella arrived back in the tunnel after helping Cool she was amazed by what she saw. Gone was the scruffy, colourless, elderly mermaid with scales missing from her tail and matted white hair.

"Wow, you look wonderful, is that really you?" she asked. The Cheerless Witch nodded and Retishella ran over to give her a big hug.

"You are so beautiful," she added, "Emerald green and sky blue all over…no longer a cheerless witch," she was lost for words.

"Retishella, my name is Sandrille, although I have not heard anyone call me by that name for many years. I would like to hear people use it again. I no longer wish to be known as the Cheerless Witch, it reminds me too much of, well, of before."

"Sandrille," said Retishella, "Your name is beautiful too."

Sandrille smiled at Retishella and it seemed as if the sun had been suddenly switched on. She had so much energy Retishella thought she could see it leaking out of every pore in Sandrille's body, like a shimmering cloud surrounding her wherever she went.

"I feel so alive, Retishella my friend. I had forgotten how much I missed the power of my cordella to restore and revive. It is a pity I cannot share it, for I would gladly use it to help you if I could."

"Sandrille, I know you would, and I thank you for thinking of it," Retishella replied. "You are so different, even your voice has changed, no longer so harsh and croaky."

Retishella looked down at her own tail, already missing some of its scales and a disgusting sludgy brown colour. She felt deep despair at the sight of it and sobbed murky brown tears. Sandrille hugged her.

"Sandrille, I must do all I can to get hold of my cordella. I must not lose sight of that landish pirate. Somehow I must force him to return my cordella to me."

Sandrille took Retishella's hand and looked deep into her eyes.

"Now that I am restored to my full powers Retishella," she promised, "I will do everything I can to help you."

The mermaids swam out into the bay hand in hand, settling down by the landish ship, which seemed to be getting ready to leave.

Chapter 19

Cool stared at the deserted beach, still covered in wreckage from the Mardy Meg, Ghastly's cliff top bonfire now just a pile of smouldering red embers in the deepening twilight.

"There's nothing left on this island," he thought to himself. "No food except for fish, and no boat to escape on, apart from the ship I see in front of me. Once it's gone I'll be stranded."

Suddenly it was clear that he had to get on to the ship. But not like the other pirates, imprisoned by armed guards; he would have to stowaway. If he could stay hidden then the next time they put into port he could escape to freedom. Maybe even help the others escape too. It was a risky plan but he had to do something.

He lowered himself into the water from a ledge of stone and swam with as much of his body submerged as possible in the direction of the ship.

As he reached the edge of the bay the sea suddenly got much colder. He felt a strong current pull at his body and as hard as he struggled against it, he found himself being dragged away from the ship and out to sea. He took a deep breath and swam with all his might in the direction of the ship but as soon as he stopped swimming hard, he was washed back to where he started. He tried again, and again, but each time he failed against the overpowering force of the currents and the tide. He was beginning to get very tired, every arm and leg muscle screamed in pain, and keeping his head above water was getting harder.

He felt himself start to sink under the water, no longer able to hold himself up, no longer able to fight against the drag of the current. He opened his mouth to scream and a rush of cold salty water stifled his voice. Then everything went black.

Chapter 20

Retishella and Sandrille floated just under the water near the ship, watching the pirates being forced on board.

"Landish people are so strange!" mused Retishella. "The ones from the ship wreck are stranded on this island, yet they are trying to avoid getting on to a ship that could help them escape."

"If I know landish people, there are some underhanded dealings going on here," answered Sandrille.

A splash and gurgling sound nearby caught their attention.

"Quick!" called Sandrille to Retishella, "Your young landish friend is drowning."

Retishella swam over to Cool who was flapping and flailing about in the water, trying to reach the ship. He was struggling against the strong current and as he rushed past her and back out to sea Retishella realised that he was not a strong enough swimmer to cope. She swam over to him as he closed his eyes and slid under the water. Tugging at his clothes she pulled him back up into the air choking and spluttering. He grabbed at her hands and steadied himself in the flowing current. He smiled weakly at her and after several deep gulps of air turned his body to look at the preparations on the ship. It was getting ready to leave.

The boy seemed very agitated. He kept pointing to the ship and saying something directly to Retishella in an urgent voice.

"He wants you to take him over to the ship," said Sandrille.

"Do you speak his language?" asked Retishella.

"No, but I speak sign language," laughed Sandrille. It looks to me like he too has realised that the ship is preparing to leave and he doesn't want to get left behind.

"I certainly can't let the landish one with my cordella out of my sight," said Retishella. The boy was signing to Retishella again, pointing to the comb holding up Sandrille's emerald green hair and then to the ship.

"I can't make it out Sandrille," she said, "What is he trying to tell us now?"

"I think he's trying to tell us something we already know. That your comb is on the ship."

"Then he realises that I still need to get my comb back," replied Retishella. "Do you think he is offering to help?"

"I don't know," answered Sandrille. "But I don't think we have many other options do we?"

The mermaids swam over to one of the rope ladders still hanging down the side of the ship and helped Cool get a foot hold. Then they hid just under the surface again and sang a song of courage and strength for the landish boy who carried all Retishella's hopes with him.

Chapter 21

As he climbed the rope ladder up the side of the ship, Cool realised he once again had reason to thank the mermaid.

"Whoever said mermaids were bad luck didn't meet mine!" he grinned.

When he reached the top of the ladder he peered slowly around. The deck was empty except for a few coils of rope and a couple of rowing boats partly covered in tarpaulins and lashed down along the stern. One of them was still wet.

He climbed aboard, dripping and shivering. By the lights on the rigging he could just about make out a cabin door in the space between the upper and lower deck, beside the nearest rowing boat.

"That is around about where I saw the pirates being forced through a door to go below decks," he thought. He crept over and peered through the porthole in the door. Behind the door was a staircase leading straight down into the hold of the ship.

Voices from the deck above stopped Cool in his tracks. Especially as one of them was Ghastly's. Cool pressed himself against the wooden wall next to the cabin door where he was out of sight of the voices. Above his head he could see through the gaps in the decking, two pairs of feet stood side by side.

"…Yes, they are all stowed safely in the hold sir," Ghastly reported to the other person, "they are securely fastened and locked in under guard, they cannot escape." Cool guessed the other person was the captain by the way Ghastly addressed him as sir.

"Very good Mr Bones. Despite losing the pirate's ship you have completed your first mission well, and will be richly rewarded when we reach St Tibor. See to it that all our merchandise arrives in good condition or our efforts will have been for nothing. And don't forget to make sure we collect up all the treasure in the caves, that is an added bonus."

The captain put his arm on Ghastly's shoulder.

"Now, how about a noggin or two in my quarters to celebrate. I would like to discuss our next project; a tea clipper that I have had my eye on for some time."

"Yes Captain, Sir. I'll just go and check on the prisoners and I'll be right there."

Cool heard their footsteps wane and their voices melt into the night air as they walked off. Here was a mystery. Why would Ghastly help anyone who wanted to capture and keep prisoner the crew of the Mardy Meg?

He looked in the porthole of the cabin door again, and finding that the coast was clear, opened it. He climbed slowly down the steps, which were more like a ladder, scarce daring to breathe.

At the bottom of the steps, he found himself in a corridor, dimly lit by candlelight in glass globes attached to the sides of the walls.

A familiar sound drifted like a whisper from the far end of the corridor.

"Music and singing; 'Hearts of Oak'," he thought excitedly. "Sounds like The Admiral still has his concertina and the crew of the Mardy Meg are in fine voice." He followed the sound and it guided him along the corridor and around a corner. He stopped and ducked into a doorway. At the far end of the corridor was a guard with a ring of keys and a sword in a leather hilt attached to his belt, standing outside a closed door.

"I bet that's the guard Ghastly was talking about, and behind that door is the crew of the Mardy Meg," he thought to himself. He looked closely at the guard, trying to work out a way to get the door open, and he realised there was something strange about him.

"He's sobbing! The Admiral was right when he said that there is great power in music."

The guard pulled a large white hanky out of his pocket and wiped both eyes with it before blowing his nose noisily.

A door opened the other end of the corridor, near the guard, and Cool bobbed behind the doorway again.

"What on earth is going on here?" Cool heard Ghastly's deep drawl followed by the sound of a slap. Cool slowly peered down the corridor. Ghastly was standing with his back towards him, looming over the guard.

"Sorry Sir," the guard replied, rubbing at a red mark on his cheek, "But the music reminded me of my home and my family. I do miss them so much." He blew his nose again and Ghastly jabbed a bony finger in his ribs.

"Call yourself a guard? Why you are no better than that cowardly lot in there. Crying is a weakness and I will not have it from the crew of this ship."

"But Mr Bones, it's been ten years since I last saw my wife and family. Ten years since Captain Rose brought me here to serve him. A man would not be human if he did not wonder what had happened to them and long to see them again."

"Silence!" yelled Ghastly so loudly that even the pirates in the locked room fell quiet. "As we are to sail on the morning tide, you shall stand guard outside the door all night and if I so much as hear a sniff you will join that repulsive crowd of pirates at the next port, although I don't expect we'll get much for you."

"Sorry sir, I won't do it again sir," said the guard standing to attention.

"That's better. Show no weakness man, that's how we get along here. Ten years on board the Pride of Beauty is a better fate than the one that your crew experienced. The same fate the crew of the Mardy Meg will soon meet."

"Yes indeed, I thank our merciful captain for saving me from that," the guard drew in a deep breath and with an effort that caused him pain, took control of his feelings. His face became blank and his eyes lost their shine but he showed Ghastly no emotions.

"That is more fitting for a guard on board this ship," Ghastly looked the guard over from head to foot. "The captain is indeed merciful. But he is not a charity. He thought you could be of help to him because you are an experienced seafarer. Don't let him down." He grabbed the guard's collar and roughly lifted his feet off the ground. "Do you understand?"

The guard choked a "yes sir," in reply. Ghastly dropped him and pushed past him. Cool caught a brief glimpse of hatred in the guard's eyes, a look he had seen before among the pirates on the Mardy Meg.

Ghastly opened a cabin door further down the corridor. He took one more look at the guard, who quickly sprang into life and stood to attention again. Ghastly entered the cabin and slammed the door shut behind him. The guard slumped and sobbed silently.

Chapter 22

Retishella and Sandrille swam all around the hull of the ship, trying to understand what was going on.

"It's very quiet in there now, Sandrille" Retishella said with a shiver, "What are they waiting for?"

"I know that these ships of wood and cloth need the wind and tide to make them move. Maybe the wind and tide are not yet right for them."

"The tide is beginning to ebb now" said Retishella. "It will not be high again until the morning, and the wind is blowing on to the shore tonight. You must be right."

"But that's good news Retishella. It gives us time to think."

"When the pirate boy had my cordella I tried to get it back by sinking his ship."

"Goodness Retishella," replied Sandrille, "How on earth did you find the strength to do that without your cordella?"

"I was very angry Sandrille. I am ashamed to say my anger took over and I didn't think it through. I wrecked the ship and nearly killed all the landish people on board."

"Yes, anger is a powerful emotion Retishella. But true strength comes from understanding and controlling your emotions."

"Yes, I know that now," Retishella said with regret. "Maybe if I hadn't lost my temper, I might have found my cordella again."

"Well, we mustn't cry over spilt bluerock juice. I have an idea." Sandrille leant closer to Retishella and spoke earnestly.

"One thing I do know is that landish people, with the possible exception of the landish boy that has been helping you, are scared of mermaids. They think we bring them bad luck. If we let them know we are here, maybe we can scare them into giving us back your cordella."

"But how will they know what we want?" asked Retishella.

"I bet your friend will soon tell them if he believes they are going to have another shipwreck," Sandrille replied.

"What do you mean?"

"I'm sure he would recognise a stormsong if he ever heard it again. We could cause just enough of a storm to scare them into thinking we are going to sink the ship."

"But I really don't have the strength any more Sandrille."

"Then my young maid it's a good job I have my cordella back. I have the strength and frustration of someone confined in that tunnel for one hundred years."

Sandrille started to sing a low, melodious tune. The seas around the ship started to bubble and the ship pitched and yawed, scraping her vast iron anchor along the seabed.

Then Sandrille changed pitch and sang high, with a voice like a violin out of tune. The wind flared up and picked at the tied-up sails, until they unfurled and flapped like crows wings in the night air.

"That'll do for starters," Sandrille smiled at Retishella. "Let's see what they think of that."

On board a voice called out a command and sailors appeared from every door, some pulling on shirts and jackets as if they had not been ready for duty. In a flurry of activity they started trying to tame and tie down the sails. They pulled up the anchor and tried several times to drop it again and safely moor the ship in the mouth of the bay. But Sandrille was ready for them at every turn.

Retishella looked up at the ship and noticed one of the important-looking sailors staring at them through a long glass tube.

"Sandrille. Be careful. They have realised we are here and are causing their trouble." But Sandrille was not yet ready to stop. She was enjoying these powerful emotions, feelings she hadn't felt for many years.

"Sandrille," called Retishella in alarm, "We must get away. They are going to kill us with their weapons." The sailors had just finished loading their guns and were aiming at the mermaids. They shot several rounds into the dark water, and despite the rolling seas and the pitching of the ship, the bullets landed like a shower of pebbles very close to Sandrille and Retishella.

"Come Sandrille. With your cordella so strong you shine brightly in the darkness. They can see you easily. We must get away." She grabbed her friend by the waist and pulled her over to hide in the rocks by the shore. The sailors were trying to work out where the sound was coming from, reloading their guns.

Sandrille changed her song. The wind changed direction and the ship started to move towards the rocks. Retishella grabbed her friend by the arms and looked into her eyes. Retishella's faced creased up with fear.

"No Sandrille, stop now. I think they have got the message. Please!"

But Sandrille's glassy stare reminded Retishella of the night she sank the Mardy Meg. She knew she didn't have the strength to snap her friend out of it. Not without her cordella.

Chapter 23

On board the Pride of Beauty Cool heard the shrieking and wailing and felt the ship lurching. Several sailors ran through the ship calling "All hands on deck!" and soon the corridor was full of sailors hurriedly pulling on their clothes and rushing on to the deck of the rolling ship.

Cool pushed open the door nearest to him. The cabin was empty; the sailors that had been sleeping there only a few minutes ago were now on deck battling with the weather. He stepped inside and peered from behind a half-closed door.

As the sailors ran by, the guard called to one of them. "Hey, Simmonds, what is going on?"

"There's a sudden squall brewing," replied a tall, blue-eyed sailor, hobbling past as he pulled on his boots. "Serious it is. Sails all a-flapping like ghosts in the night and the anchor set loose. Rumour is that there's a mermaid in the bay." With his boot securely on his foot, he swiftly climbed the stairs to join the others on deck.

Cool's mind was racing.

"I must get to Ghastly somehow. I must tell him that he could stop this storm. If I don't, this ship will suffer the same fate as the Mardy Meg."

Cool looked around the door and his eyes searched up and down the corridor. By the way the ship was heaving in the heavy storm the corridor reminded him of a fairground funhouse. But he was in no mood to laugh.

The corridor was empty except for the guard, who was no longer sobbing but was now praying. He stopped when he spotted Cool.

"Hey you!" he pulled out his sword and pointed it at Cool, staggering in the rolling ship.

Cool held up his hands. "Please, don't hurt me," he pleaded, "I know what is going on, I know how to stop all this happening."

The guard took hold of Cool and jabbed him in the back with the point of the sword.

"Tell me what you mean, pirate," he sneered.

Cool explained about Ghastly and the comb.

"Unless the mermaid gets her comb back, she will sink this ship as surely as she sank the Mardy Meg. We must get the comb back to her. We must find Mr Bones."

The guard shuddered and let Cool go. "Mr Bones won't be easy to persuade," he said.

"Where will I find him?" Cool asked.

"His cabin is down the corridor, last door on the left." The ship pitched again and they stumbled into each other. The guard watched Cool sway down the corridor for a moment, and then came to a decision.

"You cannot go alone," he said, as if he knew it wasn't a good idea, but it was the right thing to do. "Let me come with you. After all I have a weapon and you do not." Cool nodded and smiled.

"Please, one more favour," begged Cool. "My friends. Don't let them die in there like trapped animals. They are unarmed, they can do no harm. Let them take their chances with the rest of us."

"But if we get to St Tibor and have no slaves to sell, my life won't be worth living."

"They are going to be sold as slaves? What kind of terrible ship is this? I thought it was a cargo ship."

"It is. But pineapples, sugar cane and tobacco don't bring in half as much money as slave trading, so Captain Rose keeps his options open."

"You mean, he pretends to deal in pineapples, sugar cane and tobacco, but makes most of his money from catching people and selling them as slaves."

"Yes, it is true. Most of his crew are people like me who narrowly escaped being sold as slaves because they had knowledge or skills he needed. Even Mr Bones."

The sound of gunfire cracked above the whistling wind on deck.

"They are attacking the mermaids," said Cool. "We must find Mr Bones and stop this now!"

The guard put his sword back in its sheath and handed something to Cool. It was a key.

"If you open the door then I can say in all truthfulness that I didn't let the pirates out," he explained.

Cool opened the door and called to his friends.

"Hey, quickly, all of you. The ship is in danger, just as the Mardy Meg was. We need to find Ghastly. He is the only one that can save the Pride of Beauty now."

"About time you found a way to free us you tiresome tadpole."

"Thanks Captain," Cool saluted Jellycoe Jack as he and the rest of the pirates rushed through the open door.

A lurch to port and another crack of gunfire stopped everyone in their tracks.

"I know how to stop this storm," called Cool.

"Yeah, and I'm a green lollypop!" replied one of the pirates. They all laughed and climbed up the stairs to spill out on to the rain-lashed deck above.

"All hands help on deck!" called Jellycoe Jack. "When all is calm we will show these rotten rats that they can't push us about." The pirates cheered and spread across the ship like ants on a tree.

The Admiral was the only one that stayed behind.

"It's got something to do with those mermaids, hasn't it?"

"Yes," answered Cool. "We may find the answer in Ghastly's cabin. Come with me."

Cool stumbled down the corridor and tried Ghastly's cabin door. It was locked.

"You have a key," said The Admiral. "It opened our door, maybe it opens them all."

Cool nodded with a smile and tried the key in the lock. The Cabin door opened with a creak.

When they entered the cabin Cool and The Admiral realised it wasn't empty. Ghastly had stuck his gun through the porthole and was training it on the rocks where the mermaids were hidden. He fired and a long, screeching wail almost capsized the huge ship, sending them all sliding along the wooden floor. Ghastly shrieked with pain and put his hand to the breast pocket of his shirt. When he took his hand away, Cool could see it was covered in blood.

Ghastly felt the floorboard behind him creak and turned with his gun ready to fire.

Cool held up his hands.

"Mr Bones, don't shoot. I am unarmed."

"You!" Ghastly gasped. "This is all your doing. I see you have two traitors with you. Good evening to you Master Nelson and to you, Samuel. Now please leave, as you can see I am very busy."

"Mr Bones," Cool's voice wobbled with fear as he spoke, "you must give her the comb back, you must not make the same mistake as last time."

"I will not give it back," replied Ghastly. "It must be valuable to her if she will go to so much trouble and cause so much destruction to try and get it back."

"So what do you intend to do?" asked Cool, "sink the Pride of Beauty? And then what?"

"I intend to use the comb to negotiate with her people. They have power over wind and rain and sea. Just think what that is worth. I could be the most powerful human being on the planet if I could do that."

"But they can't control it, just manipulate it. She didn't want to sink the Mardy Meg; she only wanted her comb back."

Ghastly pulled the comb out of his pocket.

"It must be an important object in their world. If it wasn't she wouldn't be trying so desperately to get it back."

"It is only important to her. Not to her people. She needs it to shine like other mermaids do; I've seen it happen to her friend."

"I don't believe you boy, it can't be true."

"It is, I swear. Now take it from your pocket and give it to me."

Ghastly started to reach for his breast pocket, and then changed his mind. He lifted his gun and took aim at Cool.

"No!" the guard called Samuel shouted, flinging himself and Cool to the ground. A long moan from the mermaids outside caused Ghastly to fall to the floor screaming with pain and fire the gun at the ceiling. The Admiral rushed forward and grabbed the gun from Ghastly, while Cool and Samuel held him down and sat on him, pinning his hands behind his back so he couldn't move, no matter how he struggled.

Cool reached around and took the comb from Ghastly's blood-soaked pocket.

"I have it, I have it!" He headed for the door, turning to explain as he reached for the door handle, "I must get it to her soon."

"Where are you going?" asked The Admiral, "The porthole's open."

I can't just fling it in the sea," Cool explained, "the storm won't stop until she gets the comb back." He ran out of the door and climbed the stairs.

Chapter 24

Retishella flopped against the rocks as another round of bullets grazed past them.

"Sandrille, I really feel quite weak now. Can we stop, please?"

"Retishella, if you want your cordella back we must keep going."

"But no more shipwrecks Sandrille, no one must die. Please!"

"If you are feeling weak Retishella, leave this up to me."

Sandrille formed her mouth into a perfect 'O'.

"No Sandrille, please, don't sink the ship!"

Retishella looked out at the doomed ship. She felt helpless.

"Wait," she cried, "Sandrille, the boy, he is standing on the deck of the ship, he is holding something up high. I think it is my cordella."

Sandrille paused and took a look. As the ship rolled towards them she spotted the boy clinging tightly to the rigging and holding a small object above his head.

"We must go and have a look at least Sandrille," pleaded Retishella. She launched herself in the frothy water towards the ship.

"Stop Retishella, I bet it's just another landish trick," she called but Retishella kept going.

Sandrille pushed herself off the rocks and swam over towards Retishella.

Without Sandrille's song to keep it going, the storm began to calm, and the movement of the ship became less violent. The boy moved to the ships railing on the lower deck and leant over, trying to see the mermaids in the water.

He called something in his language.

"He's trying to tell us he has my cordella," Retishella realised. She turned to her friend. "Sandrille, he has my cordella!"

By now the seas and winds had calmed and the sailors were rushing around trying to undo the damage that the storm had done to the Pride of Beauty. All except for one.

"Boy!" Retishella called out, although she knew he couldn't understand her, "The cruel one is behind you. Look out!"

The mermaids watched in dismay as the cruel one grabbed the boy from behind, and reached out, snatching the comb from the boy's hand.

"The others are not helping," Retishella said to Sandrille, "they are gathered around watching. They are very strange people."

The cruel one had the boy pinned to the railings on the ship. The boy struggled with all his might, jumping and heaving himself up the cruel one's clothes to try and reach the comb. The cruel one

waved Retishella's cordella high up over his head in response. As the boy stretched up to grab it, the cruel one leaned over the ships rail, holding the cordella at arm's length over the swatting sea far below. The boy pulled the arm of the cruel one's coat and leaned far over the side of the ship, overbalancing and with a scream of surprise from both of them they pitched headlong over the side and into the foaming water. They landed with a splash beside Retishella and Sandrille.

"you make sure your landish friend is alright," Sandrille called to Retishella, "I'll sort the other one out." She swam over and grabbed the cruel one.

Retishella dragged the boy to safety and they sat on the rocks watching as Sandrille pinned the cruel one up against the side of the ship and sang the dream song. When the cruel one's eyes were brown and dreamy, she grabbed Retishella's cordella and was about to drop him into the water to sink like a stone.

"No Sandrille," called Retishella, "lay him on these rocks. He can do me no more harm now."

"But Retishella, he is a pitiless and spiteful human being. He deserves to die."

"You can't say who deserves to die Sandrille, you don't have that power."

Reluctantly Sandrille dumped the cruel one on to the rocks and swam back to Retishella with her comb.

As soon as she placed it in her hair, Retishella felt heat, strength and life flowing back into her body. Her eyes, hair and tail gradually filled with colour, from lime green to intense emerald. She shone like a star in the night sky. She took the boy by the hands and looked into his eyes. The bright shining light surrounded them both and in the whitest depths of it they both gained new knowledge and understanding. The light dimmed but her colour didn't. She smiled and spoke to him in his tongue, her voice like bubbly velvet.

"Thank you, I know you have placed yourself in danger to return to me what is mine. I will always be grateful to you."

"You can speak to me," he heard himself answer in the mermaid's language. "Oh this is fantastic. I wanted to thank you, for the many times you have helped us, fed us, looked after us, warned us. I'm the only one that realises how much you have done for us. Thank you kind mermaid."

"My name is Retishella, what is yours landish boy?"

"My name is Coolibar, but you can call me Cool."

They smiled.

"Please, Retishella, take me out to the ship. I don't want to stay on this bleak island any longer."

Retishella took him by the hand and they swam together out to the waiting ship.

Chapter 25

It didn't take long for Retishella and Cool to arrive back at the Pride of Beauty.

"I must help my friends Retishella, they are being held captive and are to be sold as slaves. I cannot let that happen."

"I will wait here," replied Retishella, "in case you need me." Cool climbed up the rope ladder on the side of the ship.

As he clambered back on board Cool almost collided with a huddle of pirates and crew, deep in discussion.

"Enough is enough. I did not become a sailor to spend the rest of my life slaving for a heartless captain," one of the Pride of Beauty crew announced. Several others agreed.

"We cannot allow your captain to make slaves of us, we are pirates and proud of it!" The Admiral replied.

"If we stick together we can defeat Captain Rose and get our freedom back," another sailor suggested. To a man everyone assembled on the deck agreed. They cheered and shook hands before marching off and barging into Captain Rose's cabin.

"What do you mean, coming into my cabin without so much as knocking?" he shouted, reaching for his gun at the sight of such hatred in so many faces.

"We mean to take our lives back," replied Samuel, motioning to The Admiral to get the gun. Several crew members grabbed the captain and tied his hands behind his back.

"This is mutiny," Captain Rose called out in his most ferocious voice, "You cannot do this to me. I am your captain."

"Our captor most like," answered Samuel, and the crew laughed.

"We are going to give you a choice," he continued. "My colleagues and I have decided that we are not as black hearted as you and will not kill you. We will leave you on this island to fend for yourself. That will be your punishment."

"But you can't take my ship, my cargo," Captain Rose protested.

"As far as we are concerned we are your cargo, you bullying bug," called out Jellycoe Jack. "What this here sailor says is only fair. We take your ship and your goods in return for your life. You have no choice you despicable donkey."

Before he could protest any more, the sailors and pirates lifted Captain Rose up and carried him to a waiting rowing boat. After rowing him ashore and tying him to a rock next to the sleeping body of Ghastly Bones they left the two villains on the island without a boat and set sail for the open sea.

Cool leant over the ship's rail and watched the silhouette of Obscurity Island shrink as they sailed away from the darkness of the night into the brightening dawn on the horizon. For a while he waved at the two spots of light, like two stars shining under the water, following in the wake of the ship. Then he noticed them turn away and change direction, and with a shriek of "Goodbye Cool, hope we meet again," they were gone.

Samuel gathered the crew together. "We are all crew on this ship now, no one is captain, no one is better than anyone else. I have a suggestion to make. In the morning we set sail at high tide and get as far away from this place and those villains on the island as we possibly can. At our next port of call we will sell everything, the ship, the cargo, the treasure and share what we get for it equally among us. Raise your hands if you agree."

Even Jellycoe Jack raised his hand in agreement.

"Ok then, it is agreed," continued Samuel. "Every one of us must solemnly swear we will abide by this agreement to make it binding. To show that I mean to keep my promise, I will go first; I Samuel Dorivich Barratt…"

Cool heard no more. His heart was happy enough to burst. Samuel Dorivich Barratt - that was his father's name.

Chapter 26

The next few days were a blur of excitement and happiness for Retishella too.

As she and Sandrille approached the village, she heard Sandrille give a murmur of surprise.

"It is a much bigger place than the last time I saw it," she said.

"When were you here last?" asked Retishella.

"The day I was banished for losing my cordella to a pirate captain," Sandrille smiled at Retishella.

"Then we are part of the same village, part of the same clan," gasped Retishella, "that is wonderful!"

"Your merrow, Mersia is my great-niece. Her grandmother was one of my sisters. We have never met, but I have occasionally heard of her good works. Like the time you danced with the Dolphin King and she helped you. And the time she was trapped in a block of ice by the Sneekish people. It will be good to meet her."

The two mermaids swam into the village hand in hand. Their families were ecstatic at their return and there was great rejoicing with a party that lasted a whole week, with food, dancing, storytelling, games and everything they loved doing.

Sandrille was united with Mercia, and Retishella chose them both to sit in pride of place at her welcoming ceremony.

As a thank you present, Sandrille gave Retishella a whipsilver cord, the strongest thread known, to tie her comb to her hair, so she could never lose it again.

"I'm glad I found my cordella again," said Retishella later when they sat drinking hot bluerock juice in Mersia's purple cave. "But I'm also glad I lost it."

"Why on earth would you be glad about that?" asked Sandrille.

"Because it has helped me learn so much, and it let me find you and make you my friend."

They all laughed and bubbles of joy could be seen floating on the surface of the ocean above the happy mervillage.

Lightning Source UK Ltd.
Milton Keynes UK
UKOW050045051111

181515UK00001B/1/P